Dear REMEMBRANCE

Dear REMEMBRANCE

KRITIKA G SOIN

NU VOICE PRESS

First published by NU VOICE PRESS 2025
An imprint of Hubhawks Pvt. Ltd
www.nuvoicepress.com

This is a work of fiction and all characters and incidents described in this book are the product of the author's imagination. Any resemblance to actual persons, living or dead, is entirely coincidental.

ISBN: 978-81-987421-8-6

Printed at : Manipal Technologies Limited, Manipal
Published by: Nu Voice Press

To my father, Davinder

Every little dreamer needs her wings

AUTHOR'S NOTE

❖

The concept of family has been ever evolving, to suit cultural, social, and economic requirements. Today, with rising divorces, single-parent households, and blended families, what constitutes a family is more fluid than nuclear or traditional (joint).

Dear Remembrance fleshes out the struggles of unconventional families in an Indian context. It emphasises the concept of 'chosen family' where an emotional bond is the reason to adapt to another as family, rather than a biological bond. Sometimes, it is the people we meet by chance—those who see and hold us through life's trials—who become our truest kin.

By recognising the diversity of family structures and relationships we can create a more compassionate and inclusive society.

The characters of *Dear Remembrance* are ordinary people navigating the complexities of modern life. Their thoughts, actions, and choices reflect their individual journeys, and do not necessarily represent the views of the author.

Trigger Warning: The book contains references to ragging, mental health struggles, and a suicide attempt. Reader discretion is advised.

A soul connect is all that is needed to create a family.

CHAPTER ONE

The eyes at breaking dawn
At the touch of a firefly
Shook off the slumber
Of a moonless night

IT HAD BEEN pouring through the night, reducing to a drizzle at intervals.

The shattering rain woke Smriti up from her bed. She ambled to the kitchen and prepared her ginger-lemongrass tea. She put on a mantra at a low volume, enough to surround her, and caught the words carefully in her mind.

The newspaper came in late on Sundays. The fellow probably wanted to snooze for a while longer. Smriti's building residents bonded during festivals by bickering about the late newspaper on Sundays. But with her reduced social dealings, Smriti expressed compassion for the few she interacted with. The delivery kid was young; some snoozed minutes on a Sunday would make this world an easier place for him.

She parented her plants while waiting for the newspaper and trimmed the drying ends. The overcast had softened the sunlight that reached them, and their leaves had dried up. The smell of ginger and lemongrass from the brewing tea filled her apartment.

She glanced at the ancient clock that hung on her living room wall – it was 8:30 a.m. Her agenda for the day was bifold: call Jia at 10:30 a.m. and attend the singles' support group meeting at noon.

Her phone buzzed. It was a message from Lata.

"Morning! Mohit and I are meeting up with some interesting peeps tonight, would you like to join in? I have work gossip that I'm dying to share with you!"

Smriti smiled warmly at her friend's regular prompts to go out partying.

But then she typed her equally consistent and polite refusal: *"Good morning, Lata. Thank you, but I am going to watch a film and crash early. Workday tomorrow … please carry on. I will see you next weekend. Come home on Saturday!"*

"The friend must keep trying! At least go for your support group meeting, don't skip that. And open up to others!!" Lata shot her reply. She had found out about this support group that bunched people with similar lives. Smriti had protested initially, but in acknowledgement of Lata's consistent care, she caved.

The meetings were set in a different café every Sunday and were attended by fifteen similar aged people who were either divorced, going through a divorce, or rendered widowed. Some of them were single parents, some were fighting for custody, and some had lost custodies to their ex-spouses and were living without their children. Their lives' narratives were imperfect yet unique like sea pearls, strung together by a common thread of fate.

"Yes dear, I will go! Thank you!" Smriti replied to the part about going, but not about opening up. Even after six meetings, none of them knew her story. They knew that she was a single mother, but exactly how she had come to be one …

An infrequent thought poked at her that day – had she seen all she was destined to? She brushed it off, reminding herself that her life was one she chose. She was content with how things were …

After reading the newspaper for two hours, she headed to the kitchen to prepare a simple breakfast of butter-toast and bhujia. She poured herself a second cup of chai to go along with it. At 10:30 a.m., Smriti gave Jia's boarding school a call. A few attempts later, the house mistress yelled out for Jia.

"Hello Mumma!" Jia's silvery voice warmed Smriti's heart like warm fudge. She closed her eyes to imagine Jia on the other side. Those bright hazel eyes, the curly shoulder-length hair... She tenderly replied, "Hi, *bacha*. How are you?"

"I am fine, Mummy. Was cutting my nails when you called. We have nail check every Sunday *na*," Jia replied.

"*Achha, aapka* tennis inter-house *kaisa tha?* (How was your tennis inter-house?)"

"*Array, aapko yaad hai!* (Oh, you remember!) I was the third player, so I got to play two games – *ek jeete, ek hare* (won one, lost one)," Jia shared.

"It has been raining here continuously. How is the weather in Indore?" Smriti asked.

"Here also, off and on, mostly hot. My sunscreen is over, so please courier that. I have mentioned it in my letter as well. Oh, and we got pao bhaji on Tuesday and Maggi in the mess on Thursday for dinner ... That was all that was interesting in my week," Jia added.

"*Maida* and *maida*! (flour and flour!) I read an article that said Maggi has lead. I should speak with your school about junk food," Smriti said politely, incessantly worried about Jia.

"You read the paper too much, Mom! *Kuch nahi hoga* Maggi se (Nothing will happen by eating Maggi). *Aap bhi kha liya karo kabhi kabhi!* (You should also eat it at times!) *Achha aur* (Okay, and), our quarterly exams are beginning on Thursday ..." Jia continued.

"Have you prepared well?" Smriti asked her, picking up another reason to worry about. "Beta, *padhai bahut zaroori hai* (studies are important). *Jab aur koi nahi rahega toh yehi kaam aayegi* (When no one else is by you, this is what will come to use)."

"*Dekho* (see) … I am okay in Math and English. But you know I do not understand Science … Physics, Chem, Bio fly over my head," Jia carried on.

"Never mind, you give it your best shot … and leave the rest to God," Smriti parented on.

"You and your God. Till when will you search for Him? Your life would have been different if some God was listening to you!" Jia stated her teenager opinion in her teenager tone.

"I have my prayers answered, Jia."

Jia shut her eyes for a moment before replying. "Have you made any friends apart from Lata Aunty? We don't have any relatives either. Now even I'm not at home! *Sirf office se ghar, ghar se office!* (Office to home, home to office!) And for so many years now. *Ye kaisi life hai?* (What kind of a life is this?)"

"*Main jaisi hu theek hu* (I'm fine the way I am). In fact, I had joined a single parents' support group, remember? I haven't made friends or anything … but *achha lagta hai jaa ke* (I like going there*)*. It is your time to make friends and enjoy." Smriti did not have the energy others did to make her life better – but she smiled at their jokes and enjoyed the activities they did together. The meets were adding hues, even though one could say they were pastel instead of bright ones. While continuing her chat with Jia, she glanced at the kurta set she had ironed for her day.

"*Chalo achha hai* (that's nice). At least you're going out once a week."

"How are your art lessons going on?"

"I love the exposure they have in this school for arts, Mom – landscaping, still arts, cartooning, pottery, absolutely everything. The teacher is amazing. I can stay in the art room for hours."

"Make use of the resources available to you. Learn as much as you can," Smriti guided.

"Okay Mummy, I got to go. *Aap enjoy karna apna group meet* (you enjoy your group meet). Ma'am is asking me to hang up."

"*Array paanch minute ho bhi gaye!* (Five minutes passed so soon!) Please eat well, drink your milk. I do not want to see any white spots on your cheeks the next time we meet." Smriti whispered, "I miss you."

"I miss you, Mumma. Bye-bye." As Jia hung up, Smriti's heart caved. She analyzed their call. Was she getting enough nutrition? Was she coping well with the pressures of co-curricular activities and studies? Could she study with the rushed-up routine they had in school? Did Jia want to connect more? These few minutes were unsatisfactory …

Smriti reached out to the calendar placed above the fridge and slashed another day out of it. There were three months left for Diwali – three months to loving Jia.

She readied herself for the support group meeting – placed lenses on her ebony eyes, outlined the downturn with kohl, and combed her shoulder-length salt-and-pepper strands to perfection. Jia had one feature of hers – her sharp, straight nose. The rest of Jia's features took after her father, Tushar. She brushed his memories away.

She gazed outside the window to distract herself. The rain had subsided. Meek sun rays lit the gloomy day. Smriti got into her car, a nine-year-old hatchback she was postponing selling, and drove off.

***

Keshav sat in a meeting, twisting his pen between his fingers. After dedicatedly building and selling start-ups for over eight years, Keshav was being employed by multinationals to judge their acquisitions. During his two-month work stint in Mumbai, he was invited that day to analyze the acquisition of a start-up by an FMCG company. The founder of the start-up stood before the panel and pitched the company. He finished the presentation with a slide on their estimated valuation and their proposed ask.

Keshav wrote down numbers on a notepad and passed it on to the director of the company. The director read the paper and led Keshav into a private conversation.

"It is a good investment if you get at least 33% of the stake for their ask; below that, don't invest," Keshav said.

The director communicated his offer to the start-up. A negotiation followed, and within minutes a deal was struck. The room broke into a celebration.

"The South Asian and Southeast Asian start-up ecosystems are swearing by your name now," the director said before handing Keshav his handsome check during the tea break.

Keshav nodded. "Thank you for having me."

"Until when are you in Mumbai, Mr Chopra?"

"I'm here for two more months."

"Keshav Sir, I read your book on start-up finance, it was brilliant …"

"Our Indian ecosystem needs advisors like you," the director said.

"The Indian start-up ecosystem is blossoming. I'm sure they'll see good mentors soon," Keshav replied.

Keshav gradually shuffled out of the conference room. He accepted the praises, but with a recognition of his solemn heart. It was a Sunday morning, and he was working. No matter how much he enjoyed his career, it was still a Sunday. And Sundays were meant for something else. For something he did not have – *family.*

He sat back in the taxi, took out his phone, and dialed his ex-wife Neha's number to speak with his son, Kaveer.

"Hi Neha, is Kaveer home?" he asked, as was routine.

"He's out with his friends playing cricket," she said.

"There is always an excuse, Neha. I've been calling for three days continuously to speak with my son, and you've not had the courtesy to call back."

"He's growing up now, Keshav, he stays busy." Neha had not always been curt.

"You've become so rude, Neha. Why can't we be cordial? No matter how busy and grown up, you have to make us speak with one another, I will always be his father –"

"Yes, I'm no longer the twenty-year-old who fell for you. I've seen life now. Listen, Keshav, I'm getting another call. I'll call you back when Kaveer is home," Neha cut him short and hung up.

Keshav leaned deeper into the luxury cab's leather seat. He loosened his tie and undid the top button of his office shirt.

I feel tired early in the morning, he thought.

He glanced at his wallpaper. It was a picture from Kaveer's previous visit. They'd gone bowling and won a game against another father-son duo. He smiled at the memory. Kaveer had grown up now. Every time he visited Keshav, he was inches taller.

He was pulled into another flashback – Neha and a younger Kaveer leaving their apartment. Neha was calling out for Kaveer, asking him to hurry up; Kaveer was crying.

"I don't want to live away from you Papa, and I don't want to live in India." Young Kaveer's words were etched into Keshav's memory.

It was the second worst day of his life …

A call broke his chain of thoughts. It was Mahesh, his school friend.

"Are you done with your meetings? Made your millions?" Mahesh said jokingly.

"Very funny, Mahesh. Yes, I'm done," Keshav replied.

"Did you speak with the adoption agency yesterday?" Mahesh asked.

"Yes, they won't entertain a single man. I know you'll say you told me so, but finding out first hand was worth a shot …" Keshav said. "Anyway, this Neha, she acts pricey all the time … It is a task to speak with Kaveer through her."

"Sue her! Take her to court! It'll be fun … we'll take all of Kav's custody … and then bother her," Mahesh said jokingly.

"Your idea of fun has been creepy since school …" Keshav mocked and teased Mahesh out of habit.

"Shut up, you miss my creepy sense of humor in Singapore, don't you?" Mahesh continued the banter.

"Listen, why has it been raining ever since I've come! So gloomy … I'm missing Singapore's sun!" Keshav said solemnly. It was easier to say that the weather was gloomy rather than his life.

"I can't do anything about our sexy rains, but I can bring in sunshine … I'm coming to pick you up in thirty minutes, SUIT UP!" Mahesh, his friend, directed, quoting Barney Stinson from *How I Met Your Mother*.

"But for what?" Keshav asked.

"My support group meet!" Mahesh replied.

"What will I do in your support group, Mahesh?" Keshav asked, surprised.

"Well, find support, some company. Mingle, reduce your loneliness…"

"Are you sure I can come along? I have two months in Mumbai. Any company I provide would be fleeting," Keshav stated.

"Don't give me all that. I've spoken with the facilitator. They're happy to have you! I'll see you in thirty!"

***

Smriti tuned into her unvarying choice of ghazals. After driving through flyovers, she reached the café. She spotted a parking space. As she was about to position her car, another car overtook her sharply and dived for the parking slot. She waited to see who got out of the car. It was Mahesh. She shook her head and changed the gear to drive on toward another slot.

Mahesh saw Smriti's car passing by and grinned mischievously at her.

Keshav got down from the car and joined Mahesh. He shook his head from side to side, disapproving of Mahesh's mannerisms, and chided him, while Mahesh gloated. Smriti stopped her car to watch him from the rear-view mirror.

Snapping out of her distraction, Smriti parked the car and walked to the café.

Five of the fifteen had reached. The rest were pouring in.

A long table was set up for the group. Smriti walked in behind Mahesh and Keshav.

"Aha, sorry Smriti!" Mahesh grinned like a college kid, his sharp features radiating excitement from having won the parking slot from her.

Smriti smiled and took her seat. "It's alright," she said.

"He's in some mood today! What happened Mahesh? Is Ishita letting go of her alimony? Case closing?" asked a middle-aged lady named Seema. Seema had lost her husband three years ago. She had signed up for the support group around the same time as Smriti.

"*Array kahaan aisi kismat* (I'm not that lucky!), to marry her I had to combat my family, and now to divorce her I have to combat the courts. This lady has been a *panauti* (trouble) in my life! Anyway, my mood is good because of my buddy here! Meet Keshav, guys – my school friend! He's here for a work project and will be joining in for two months. He is a big shot in Singapore *haan*. And, ladies, *mera bhai single hai* (my brother is single)!" Mahesh winked at the women around him, becoming a wingman for his friend.

Tall, heavy-shouldered, with a belly that bulged farther than his chest, Keshav was a hearty man. His Indian-gold skin tone and sharp Punjabi features were magnified by the genuine smile he passed to those at the table. The roots of his dyed hair were washed gray; his hairline stretched backward to show signs of balding.

Something about his appearance was … cheerful.

"Hi Keshav. We are glad to have you. You may introduce yourself once everyone is here," said Samir, the charming forty-eight-year-old widower who facilitated the support group.

The café bustled with energy as the middle-aged combatants of marriage and life exchanged greetings and jokes. Smriti was quiet.

Samir sat at the head of the wooden table and guided the café attendant to take everyone's food and beverage orders.

"Juhi, do you want to share how the meeting with your ex-husband was?" Samir asked with a smile while everyone settled down.

"I realized that it was a fair decision to leave him! He reached almost an hour late; the kids were so irritable by then. People do not change, do they? I am glad I have to put up with it occasionally now!" Juhi sighed.

"You do seem happy!" Samir replied. He waited till everyone was seated before introducing Keshav. "Hey guys, we have someone new with us. Keshav, right?"

Keshav's friendly broad hand reached out to people across the table.

"Keshav, would you like to share your story with everyone?" Samir continued.

He nodded. An angel-like light emitted from his brown almond-shaped eyes. His heart plunged as he decided he was going to say the truth out, without any filters. No matter how hard, he was going to share *his story*.

He cleared his throat to speak, took a deep breath, and looking down at the table, expressed:

"My name is Keshav. I got divorced a few years back. We did not drag the process. Though we began fighting right after the honeymoon phase, it was after the –" his voice simmered low, "after the – loss of my two-year-old daughter – she was my second child, that things went downhill. I tried to be there for my wife, uh, ex-wife, but she never acknowledged it. I was not given space and time to grieve, it was always about her. Our relationship turned toxic, and eventually we had to part ways. My older child, Kaveer, fourteen now, is with her in Kerala. We meet twice a year during holidays."

His voice dropped to a simmer. He looked down at the table, fiddling with his frothy coffee glass. His chest swelled up. He wanted to admit that he missed his children. He wanted to break down in the company of this compassionate group of people that had similar lives. While consoling his wife and caring for her, his cup had emptied. No one had been there to ask him if he was doing alright.

"He lost a daughter …" Seema whispered under her breath.

"He lives without both his children ..." added another member in a murmur.

Smriti was sitting two spots away on the opposite side. As she saw Keshav, a stranger, admit his suffering, her throat went dry and her chest tightened. She placed her fingers on her heart, *grief* ... any emotion was new to Smriti.

Keshav's eyes met Smriti's. A sense of stability radiated across the table to meet his brimming emotions. He held tears back. He nodded to acknowledge the comforting impact she had.

He smiled, looking around, comforting the group as they settled with the truth of his life.

In a matter of minutes, he was settling in with the cohort again. He attempted jokes with Mahesh, nudging forward from his introduction. His aura carried a childlike innocence that dreamt of happiness again.

Though Keshav was chatting with others, his eyes darted back to notice Smriti's simplicity. The salt-and-pepper-haired woman had unknowingly consoled him.

As the meeting went on, a group of four women were discussing how their lives were affected by their cooks – one was light-heartedly complaining about how after the divorce, their spouse took away their decade-old cook; another lady had caught her husband bathing with the male cook, bringing him out of the closet after fifteen years of a heterosexual marriage, and another had severe fights since her cook was made to report to her mother-in-law even though she lived in another city; for another, the cook's personal matters had once brought the police into the apartment.

Two people chatted about how anxious they were at night; insomnia was hitting hard. A group of four was laughing over Mahesh's and Keshav's jokes – their inability to date without thinking about the alimony it could amount to.

Smriti heard their jokes from a distance, but kept to herself.

Minutes back he spoke about his personal life. How is he so chirpy? she thought.

"How was the call with your daughter today, Smriti?" Juhi asked her, breaking her thoughts.

"It was good, Juhi. She is learning tennis these days. I worry about her meals though!" Smriti said, reminiscing the phone call.

"There is nothing like *maa ke haath ka khaana* (home-cooked food cooked by a mother), no!" Juhi smiled. "I still cook for my kids, even after a rough work day."

"A mother's energy is the closest to God's …" Smriti said, smiling gently and cutting the conversation short.

After a while, Samir took charge of the bustle and unified them with their weekly activity.

"Paints and brushes are before you; you have to paint the canvas with your non-dominant hand," Samir said.

"ARE YOU SERIOUS? I don't remember using my left hand for anything!" exclaimed Tuhina, a fifty-year-old, who wore her golden-colored pixie haircut gorgeously. She was the oldest in the group but could pass for the youngest.

"That is why you have got to use it to paint! It will help you unravel your inner child, your subconscious. Did you know, using your non-dominant hand can delay dementia? We want to better our mental health, no?" Samir explained with a wide grin, taking charge fluently.

"I do not think I have done anything this adventurous. I mean it, I did skydive three months back, but this is chilling," said Keshav anxiously. He laughed with his peers as he picked up his paintbrush like it was an unfamiliar weapon.

They drew long breaths as they looked at the canvas which, unlike their lives, tainted with memories and muddles, was blank, ready for them to spoil and celebrate.

They pulled up their sleeve ends, picked up brushes with their non-dominant hands, and dipped them into paint.

Smriti painted trees. Keshav painted the sea. Mahesh painted his canvas black. Juhi painted the sun and a cat. Samir painted a rainbow. The others painted their version of the moment.

In a moment of silence that befell the group, Smriti hummed the tune of the Rafi song she was listening to in her car. It was still playing at the back of her mind. The non-dominant hand trick unleashed it.

"Likhe jo khat tujhe … woh teri yaad mein …"

Sitting spots away, Keshav heard it, smiled, and sang the following line of the song out loud,

"Hazaaro rang ke, nazaare bann gaye …"

Taken back by her audaciousness, Smriti flushed red.

"Not bad, not bad!" Samir said, adding his voice to their jingle.

Gradually, the group of fifteen, in a jangling, unmelodic manner, began singing, *"Likhe jo khat tujhe … woh teri yaad mein … hazaaro rang ke, nazaare bann gaye …"*

It was unlike her to attract attention. She glanced at Keshav and nodded. He met her eyes and smiled tenderly.

The meeting ended on a high for Smriti, for she had known the fireflies of wonder.

CHAPTER TWO

The mirth,
The skipped beats,
The light,
Is this what spring looks like?

LATA STOPPED BY Smriti's house for dinner on Saturday. She waltzed into the house in an embellished blue shirt and white pants.

"Cute shirt, Lata," Smriti said as Lata settled herself at the dining table.

"These shirts are in vogue – Indian designers are adding embroidery to western shirts. Shall we get you one next Sunday? I can book an appointment with the designer. Her store is in Juhu."

"*Array* no, I have so many clothes. It will only add to the closet pile," Smriti said. She prepared the last laccha parantha and placed it in the casserole. She laid the table with her archaic china.

"Why did you have to cook all by yourself?" Lata asked, looking at the wholesome meal laid out for her. "Who has time in Mumbai to cook all this for two people, Smriti! So much *magajmari* (botheration). We could have gone out *toh*!"

"That would have taken me more effort than cooking at home!" Smriti replied.

"At least we could have ordered in!" Lata replied, pouring daal makhani into her bowl and taking a bite.

Smriti passed her the casserole of paranthas.

"Actually, this was a great idea! These paranthas are melting in the mouth, Smriti! Man, Savitri didi doesn't cook half as well! No wonder Jia misses your cooking. Is she doing okay at school?"

Jia's letter had come in earlier that evening. Smriti had put it aside to read later on. She glanced at it and then said, "She is doing fine … enjoying her art classes."

"Best thing about these boarding schools is their extra-curricular. How is your support group coming along? Offering you any support?" Lata asked, raising her eyebrows, while digging into the meal.

"I don't need support!" Smriti replied, her fluttery eyes cloaking the sliver of doubt she experienced off and on.

"Till when would I be your only friend? Did you meet anyone you could hang out with? We have no one to gossip about! Anybody sizzling hot? Or not – an average could work well!"

Smriti gulped.

"There was this guy in the previous meeting –"

"Aha, finally, a guy … way to go!" Lata pursued with vigor. "I'm excited for you, Smriti!"

"We haven't even spoken yet! I don't know if I intend to – I found him … inspiring. He's gone through a lot in his personal life, and yet he doesn't seem as numb … as me," Smriti opened up. The consistent sorrow, loss of faith, another child to explain to where his sibling had vanished. But his spirit defeated his story. How?!

"Inspiring is a start …" Lata motivated her friend. "It's a start …"

Smriti diverted the topic from her and into Lata's life. Lata was a senior in a PR agency, and most of her clients were in Bollywood. Her routine was filled with drama.

"I had to work on Sunday. One of my clients got into trouble with the media. Every time this fellow gets a contract, word gets around and people start spreading rumors. I'm not saying the rumors don't have a basis, but we have worked so hard at maintaining his privacy … Why should what one does with their love life affect their career? You do know who I'm talking about, right? He was all over the weekend news."

Smriti shook her head. She usually tossed away the film section of the paper.

"Yeah, of course you don't know. Has my friendship had any effect on you? Never mind. Anyway, so the team was called up to clear the mess. I missed being home on Sunday. What was worse was that by the time I got home, Mohit was off with his friends. Avantika was so irritable with our preoccupations. I had to manage her by taking her to this fancy restaurant that serves these teeny tiny portions; her friends had been recommending it to her. My life literally revolves around riot and chaos management," Lata continued.

Smriti laughed. "Our lives are so different, Lata. How is Avantika doing?" she asked.

"She's taking after her father, wants to hog desserts all day," Lata stated. "I am mothering two children, cautioning one about cavities and the other about diabetes."

Father, Smriti thought solemnly, looking away from the dining table toward the window. While Lata spoke of her life, Smriti observed her plants. The leaves glistened under the living room lights. She had planted them as seeds – the flower plants – blue pea, mogra, the herbs – tulsi, basil, ajwain, pudina and a few just-like-thats. She used the leaves in her everyday cooking.

"If I tell her not to binge on junk, she comes up with body shaming dialogues. She's ten, what all is she learning? Also, I'm afraid she's keeping company of snooty kids in school, she was asking me how much a trip to Spain costs." Lata paused for Smriti to pitch in, but upon getting no reply, she continued, "How do I keep her grounded, Smriti? Grounded and healthy! You're the parenting expert!" She went on, "Smriti … where are you lost?"

"I'm sorry. Nowhere, I'm right here. Avantika is eleven, right? Send her to classes where she can make friends from diverse backgrounds … some volunteering on weekends … maybe you guys can do it together as a family!" Smriti replied, coming back from her daze.

"One of my clients volunteers to maintain her reputation. Maybe I can ask her …"

Smriti nodded and smiled.

"Don't you get bored at home every day? Why don't you join us? At least volunteering is something you'd enjoy."

Smriti thought about it for a moment. Volunteering with Lata's family could be a nice outing for her. "Maybe when Jia is back from school, we both can join your family," she said and half-accepted the offer.

The monsoon breeze caressed the apartment, filling the space with the scent of the city.

"Your apartment is so peaceful," Lata said.

Smriti put on music on the Caravan. Lata chatted over the music.

After Lata left, Smriti dived into Jia's letter. It was written with the stationery they had shopped together before Jia left for boarding school.

Hello Mummy,

How are you? I have made three friends in school - Anya, Mishika, and Srishti. They are sweet to me and the four of us have formed a group, called the JAMS. Anya has a baby sister; she keeps her picture under her pillow while sleeping. She misses her. We get our discman during the weekend and I listen to my music till I doze off.

A few girls have created a strong group together and they have sisters in senior batches, making them big bullies. They bully my friend Srishti. They are mean to her and have boycotted her completely. They steal things and put the blame on her, and they throw her things in the dustbin, wet her clothes when she has to wear them, etc.

These days our teachers are giving us plenty of homework. Geography is interesting - we are learning this topic called topography. We hardly get time to finish our homework since there are inter-house competition practices at night. I'm looking forward to the Art & Craft competition - dates aren't announced yet. I try to study with the torch at night after the competition practices, but sometimes our matron catches us and gets angry that we are up past bedtime. What to do - study or sleep!

We have philosophical conversations these days among us - you know, about life and all. Everyone has such distinctive viewpoints, it is interesting. What do you think is the purpose of life, Ma?

Two pairs of my socks and one undergarment have gone missing - please courier them to me. And, I need sunscreen.

On Saturday evening, our House watched an animated movie together.

How is your work life? I hope you are not missing me too much. I lent some of my stickers to my friends so they could decorate their letters.

I miss you, Mummy.

Love,

Jia

Smriti put down the letter with glistening eyes. She picked up her pen and letter-pad to write. She wrote back to Jia, asking her about meals, games, and advising her to stay away from the bullies.

Remember what Mufasa tells Simba in *The Lion King* story: "Being brave does not mean that one should go looking for trouble."

She pondered over the philosophical discussions taking place in a teenager dormitory. What could she tell her fifteen-year-old girl about the purpose of life?

She chewed at the end of her pen, finding herself at a crossroads – she could either tell Jia that life was not a bed of roses, it played by itself and any discussion as to the purpose of it would be futile … or that life was beautiful, through its ups and downs. With either of the answers, Smriti would not be doing justice.

For most of it, the reins of her life had not been in her hands. Life had happened along.

So instead, she chose to write:

Beta, sometimes what we are doing is asking the wrong question. Life is a culmination of many days and many moments. If we look to define the purpose of life, we drown the purpose of those moments. Life falls in place when the beauty behind each moment is recognized. There is no target to chase, no end to attain, no purpose to define existence. You should experience each day, see what it brings, let things unfold, and practice to perceive your life as a glass half-full.

I found purpose in spending time with you - feeding you, watching you laugh, getting you ready for school, watching you grow, travelling with you - my purpose was formed in the tiny memories I've made with you. If life is a surprise, it's purpose should be too …

Smriti paused, rotated her pen between her fingers, dropped it, touched her forehead, and continued…

`Jia, at a crossroads, always choose the path which makes you feel lighter, which detangles … when you take each step at a time with belief in your heart, the dots, looking back, will connect. A purpose would have formed, looking backward …"`

She sealed the letter to courier the next day, thinking about how impressionable Jia's mind was at the time. She wondered if having an incomplete family still bothered her.

She never speaks to me about it, Smriti thought.

***

"The sales are increasing but our customer acquisition is high. We aren't seeing as many repeat buys as we expected. Business Development has burnt a deep hole. When do we see a break-even for this? It has been three years in red." A start-up founder sat with Keshav, worried about the company's numbers.

Keshav rubbed his forehead. *They are trapped and the only way out is another angel investor,* he thought. *But he'll drown more money if he gets it.*

"Add another product line," Keshav said. "A product that would add value to the same niche market. Capitalize on your business development through product lines. It should be an ancillary product, which can be added in the same cart by a repeat customer. Don't spend more on R&D or on setting up the supply chain."

"Shouldn't we look at another angel investor?" the start-up founder asked anxiously, proving Keshav's hunch right.

"Not at all! I helped you get the investment because I believed in you. I thought you'd work harder than this. Don't drown money! You young kids want things easy. Investors are investing, not donating. Make the company work, Harsh!"

"Yes, Sir…" Harsh gathered his scattered documents and scuttled out of Keshav's office.

Keshav buried his face in his hands. While on most days he loved his work – working on ideas that were the building blocks of tomorrow, there were some days he found his work futile. Because the reality was that very few start-ups found success. A majority were struggling because of weak management and lack of dynamism. The bubble was getting larger, and he was a part of it.

Most of them have left their secure careers to build start-ups; they'll be doomed if they don't operate sensibly and vigorously, Keshav thought. There had to be a way to navigate this. He needed to figure out how to create better entrepreneurs and leaders, not just start-ups with potential.

He poured himself a scotch on the rocks and ordered in a meal. While waiting for his meal, he checked out Neha's phone number.

She'll give me some excuse again.

Keshav shut his eyes. He let a minute pass, and then another … till the delivery guy rang his cell for the third time.

He took the delivery. The emptiness of his office loomed over him.

I hate eating alone, he thought. He fetched out a picture of himself with his late daughter, then swiped to a family picture of all four of them. He ate his dinner with the picture laid out.

His phone buzzed with Mahesh's text: *"Will pick you up tomorrow at 11:30 a.m."*

"It does not make sense for me to come," Keshav replied.

"Stop with these protests," Mahesh texted, *"it is still raining, you do need sunshine, don't you?"*

***

Wearing a Lakhnavi kurta, Smriti reached the support group meeting early. Only Samir was there.

"Hey, Smriti! You've come early to get the easiest parking slot no!" Samir grinned.

"Yes Samir, hi!" Smriti replied in a sincere monotone. "What activity have you planned for us today?"

"Oh, I intend to keep that a surprise," he replied. "How's your daughter?"

"She is alright. I spoke with her in the morning …" Smriti said.

Tuhina joined in. Her purple lenses added another layer to her edgy appearance.

"Hi Tuhina! Wow, you're wearing colored lenses!" Samir said.

"Yeah. I can fight the body's age in the day, not in the night. No amount of meditation or chamomile teas have been working for me. I sleep terribly, tossing and turning. All morning, I was waiting for the clock to strike noon so I could come here … and wear purple lenses." Tuhina told Samir. She hung her neon-colored purse at the edge of her chair and took her seat.

"Same for me. Last I slept well was when Rohini slept next to me …" Samir said.

They both have lost their spouses, Smriti thought. *Life is hard for everyone* …

As members joined in, Smriti shied away into her thoughts, recalling her chat with Jia in the morning:

"I read your letter. It spoke of the bullying. I hope they have not been bullying you, beta. Please let me know if they are."

"No, Mom, they are not bullying me," Jia whispered into the phone, her voice croaky and broken.

"Are you alright?" Smriti asked again.

"Yes Mom, I have a cough. It is running through school. My entire batch has it. They are in and out of the infirmary," Jia explained, "My matron has quit. She was kind. I don't know how the new one will be …"

Jia has cough … Smriti thought, *how did she get it? It must be the changing weather.*

Mahesh and Keshav walked in. Keshav asked if he could sit in the chair beside her. With a bowed head, Smriti nodded.

"Keshav," he announced in his kind voice, extending his hand.

"Yes, I remember your introduction from the previous session. I am Smriti." Smriti returned the shake and allowed him to take the seat beside her.

"Smriti … what does it mean?" Keshav asked.

"Umm … Smriti referred to that part of the Vedas that could be remembered or memorized, as opposed to the Shruti texts, which were divinely revealed. When using the word generically or poetically, Smriti means to recall an emotion … the nostalgia of a past experience … simply put, remembrance," Smriti explained meticulously and in a flat tone.

"Oh, that sounds … pretty. I will surely 'remember' it! My name is an expression of Lord Vishnu's divine love and wisdom. But you know what Keshav indicates? One with long, luxurious hair – ironically, look at my hairline!" Keshav joked, running his hand through his receding hairline.

Smriti let out a free-spirited laugh.

Keshav observed her – her perfectly groomed, short, monochrome hairstyle, her unpierced ears, her deep ebony eyes that held a sense of submission to life, her tall neck, and her collarbone showing through the aging skin.

His stare had been longer than hers. He broke the connect to initiate conversations with others.

"This time Mahesh almost stole another's parking. I had to wrestle him to stop. Hey, what is with you, Mahesh?" he asked, chuckling.

"It is his desire for power struggle. Must be missing fighting with his wife! Side effects of separation, no? We do not know who to fight with anymore. No longer have our punching bags … Life is bland. Right, Mahesh? I am going through something similar, so I understand your need to steal parking lots," Juhi, who was taking a seat herself, blurted out.

"Haan *yaar,* Juhi. Never imagined I would miss the bickering; the house can get quiet, especially in the evenings," said Mahesh.

"You have not seen holidays yet, right? Festivals are the worst. I live in Singapore – though work takes up time and mind-space – my apartment is lonely!" Keshav shared as the group settled in. He raised his eyebrows to acknowledge Smriti's presence and invite her into the conversation.

"I've no experience of marriage," Smriti stated in response to Keshav's statement.

"Really? None?" Keshav asked, raising his eyebrows in surprise this time. "You've never been married?" he asked again, his voice filled with compassion.

Smriti shook her head.

He caught the vibe that she was a private person. "By the way, have you shared your story with everyone here?" he asked, taking a leap.

"No … I do not think I have it in me to tell so many people. In fact, it was brave of you, to tell everyone," Smriti confided, looking at Keshav with awe.

"You should share … Everyone is here for mutual support. No one is going to judge," Keshav convinced her. "Unless of course you murdered the father … Not a criminal the police is looking for lah? If that is the case, please keep your story to yourself; we will be treated as accomplices if we know about it!" Keshav joked and Smriti let out a chuckle.

"No, no. Nothing like that." Smriti smiled from her heart. "It's a simple story …" she said, staring into space.

"Go ahead then. Keeping it within you is doing damage, trust me … open up …" Keshav suggested sweetly. "Will you?"

Smriti smiled bleakly. "I am not sure I can. I have never spoken to anyone about it before."

"In that case, you must talk it out. Share as much as you are comfortable sharing. Speak one sentence at a time, and let it flow," Keshav advised.

"What good will it do?" Smriti questioned apprehensively.

"It will make you feel lighter, dear *Remembrance*," Keshav said.

Something about Keshav's warm eyes made her want to trust him, even though she hadn't trusted anyone in years.

Smriti nodded modestly.

He saw that everyone had settled into their seats. "Hey Samir! Smriti here has something to share with everyone today!" Keshav nudged Samir privately.

Smriti glanced at Samir, who nodded a go-ahead, and then skimmed through the fifteen people seated before her. Her heart was beating fast, beads of sweat forming on the nape of her neck. She had never spoken about what happened fifteen years back.

She took another look at Keshav, mouthed an "okay", and geared herself for her narrative.

She clutched the hems of her kurta and closed her eyes to recall the memory she had buried away.

"I was twenty-two, I made the mistake of falling for the wrong boy." Smriti paused, opening her eyes; looking down at the desk, she continued. "We dated for three years. When I got pregnant, he left me. I contacted him, told him … but he sent a note through my friend saying he wanted nothing to do with us," Smriti confessed into the space more than to those around her. People blurred as she went on. "It was a scary time. I remember howling so much in the first trimester that I needed to rush to the hospital … I was by myself … My parents cut contact with me … I have not visited those memories again …" Smriti dug her face into her palms before she continued. "Faced judgement, harassment, while I raised her by myself …"

She paused for a while, looking ahead, across the people surrounding her, at the wall. She let the trapped energy of her heart bubble out into the universe.

"I contacted him. He still does not want anything to do with us … even with my, uh, our daughter," she submitted in a low volume.

She closed her wet eyes; tears rolled down her cheeks.

"The worst is, I am not sure of the impact it has had on her … I have never had sufficient answers for her … She was conceived by mistake … and … I think she is still looking for an answer I don't have myself." Smriti shook her head from side to side. "I wonder what she tells her friends …" Her chin trembled as she held herself back.

The group sat in silence, absorbing her story.

Seema, sitting next to Smriti, stroked her back. "We're with you," she said.

"We're with you Smriti," they whispered, following Seema's cue.

"I am sorry. We are proud of you," Keshav whispered.

"Thank you." Smriti locked gaze with the kind eyes that had pushed her into opening her personal Pandora's Box. His kindness rubbed off on her.

She went to the restroom and cried. Looking at the mirror, she thought, *I have been in the same situation, thinking and feeling the same things for years now … So much time has passed by, Jia is fifteen now …*

She splashed water on her face and went back to join the group.

Keshav was right, she did feel lighter. A stiffness was vacuumed from her chest.

"Are you ok?" Keshav asked when she came back.

Smriti nodded as she took her place. "Yeah. I have forgotten those rough years, but they're still a part of me somewhere, you know." She had spoken more than she expected herself to.

"Of course they are a part of you. Keeping emotions bottled up would have been difficult. You will feel better now, I am sure of it," Keshav said gently.

"By the way, why did you never marry? Don't you wish you had explored that side of life?" Keshav asked her in a volume that only Smriti could hear, letting the others continue with their conversations.

"Maybe at some point I did. But I was busy raising her and was unsure of the impact it would have on her upbringing. I did not know how to do it … like, balance between my daughter and someone new … I do not think of it anymore. It will be a hassle – my daughter is fifteen. It is her age to date," Smriti disclosed solemnly.

"It might be her age to move ahead in life, but that does not mean it is not your time to live! Your life is no less important – *Zindagi Na Milegi Dobara,*" he said with a smile.

She noticed that the edges of his eyes were crinkled up, as if he were always smiling. A flutter swam up through her stomach into her throat.

"Hey, hey! We congratulate Yuvraj on finding a mate," Samir announced, interrupting the conversation between Keshav and Smriti.

Yuvraj raised his hand to show his wedding band. "And to my ex-girlfriend from school!" he said out loud, his round eyes shimmering with excitement.

"It was always meant to be, then!" said Tuhina.

"Shouldn't we be drinking champagne today then, Samir?" Mahesh got his wits out.

"You know we don't drink at our meet-ups, Mahesh!" Samir said with a straight expression.

"Yuvraj, you should take us out after this then!" Mahesh continued with his entertainment.

"I'll call all of you for my engagement party," Yuvraj said.

"Yeah, fifteen middle-aged singles will cheer for you on your engagement," Mahesh commented sarcastically.

Keshav and Smriti went back to their private chatter.

"I have been open to meeting people, but it has gotten tougher to find compatibility. Everyone is guarded and inhibited. It is not as easy to find companionship as it was in the younger years," Keshav opened up.

"I have not missed out on anything then, correct?" Smriti asked with a smile and raised eyebrows.

"No, you have missed, if you consider quest or hope as life … To hope is to live," Keshav replied. "And the hope for true love … well, that is life's grandeur, magnificence."

I had written something similar in Jia's letter, being open to life brought it purpose, Smriti thought.

Smriti glimpsed at him with a glint in her eyes, her knots unwounded.

"What work do you do in Singapore?" Smriti made the simpler conversations.

"I work in the start-up ecosystem. I was a management student. I moved to Singapore for a job opportunity. About four odd years back, immediately after my divorce was settled, I took the leap of having a tech-based start-up. I sold that one, then another and another. Soon I was associated with ten start-ups. Kept selling. I have been a founder, an angel investor, a lot on advisory …"

"You love what you do." Smriti sighed.

"I do; I love my work. I'm facing some bottlenecks … but I love it. How about you? Do you not like your profile?" Keshav asked.

"No, it is a boring desk job, data analysis – offshore accounts. But I have to do it to provide for my daughter," Smriti submitted another truth into this friendship.

"What would you rather have done in life?" Keshav asked.

Discovering herself through their conversation, Smriti blurted, "I guess I would have taught children. Or maybe some craft … I don't know!"

Samir announced, "Activity time guys, get into pairs today! We have called a chef today."

"Are we going to try to make sushi?" A lady who went by the name Usha beamed with excitement as the ingredients were placed before them. Usha enjoyed wearing ethnic sarees. She had worked with the ikkat handicraft industry.

"Yes, Usha. It's a sushi-making class," Samir declared.

Keshav and Mahesh grinned like high-school boys shrugging off homework.

"Team up with me," Keshav asked Smriti.

"Bro?" Mahesh smirked across to him, let down by his partner-in-crime.

"Are you fond of sushi?" Keshav asked Smriti. "What was your first experience of trying wasabi? Do you remember it?"

"I've had it, maybe thrice! I mix the wasabi in the soy and then pour it on my sushi. It lessens the strength and evenly distributes it," Smriti explained with details.

Keshav laughed. "The wasabi is the fun part, why do you dilute it?"

"Because I am not fun," Smriti said, explaining how she was fond of routine and stuck to the ordinary.

"I think anyone who meets you can sense that. We need to shake you up." Keshav motioned a shaking gesture with his hands.

"You've already done enough of that today. And now, we have to make sushi here." Smriti made eye contact as she collected their ingredients.

They followed the steps to make sushi, and both of them failed miserably.

"Juhi and Tuhina seem to be doing a decent job. What is with the butter fingers, guys?" Samir asked the noisy teams.

Keshav cut the vegetables unevenly, and as they tried to roll it, the sushi cracked. The vegetables jutted out of the roll. Keshav picked out a jutting cucumber with his chopstick and put it in his mouth.

"Stop eating it!" Smriti said, handling the *nori* sheets terribly herself.

"We are anyway making a mess of it!" Keshav chuckled. "But wait, I will turn it around. Keshav Chopra is no loser. Let's create a story around it. Let's call our sushi rolls … the Deconstructed Sushi!"

Smriti placed the rolls on the plate and cut them into proportioned pieces. "Careful, careful Smriti …" she whispered out loud as she concentrated hard. She picked up the sushi with her chopstick and it fell over.

This is difficult! she thought and placed her fists on her waist. "Keshav's and Smriti's Risky Rolls!"

"Ooh, that's a better name for it! See, you are learning to be funny in my presence!"

Smriti looked at him, smiled, and rolled her eyes. She quickly noted down the name on a placard and placed it in front of their sushi plate.

"Hey Samir, check out our sushi. We call them the Risky Rolls," Keshav said. "As risky as the mid-life crisis!"

"Good last-minute addition!" Smriti added in a murmur.

"You named your sushi!! Are you kids?" Mahesh jested.

Samir looked over at their plate and laughed. "I would have given today's prize to both of you for your efforts to name your sushi rolls …"

"But? Where's the but?" Smriti asked.

"But Juhi and Tuhina's perfect rolls deserve due credit."

Juhi and Tuhina high-fived each other. Smriti and Keshav exchanged a look.

"Marketing can only take you so far …" Keshav said with a frown.

"Thank God they lost! Silly businessman trying tactics to win!" Mahesh teased.

"Well, at least we have a fun memory!" Keshav replied to Mahesh. "That's enough as a consolation prize!"

This is the most fun I have had in a long time, Smriti thought. The sun on her side of the world shone brighter that day.

She spent the remainder of her Sunday grocery shopping and thinking about the afternoon. She had never picked up the phone and ranted about her day to anyone. And she hadn't laughed that way in years.

Keshav was right, Smriti thought, her body feeling lighter. *If I could guide Jia to believe, why did I stop believing in my life?*

CHAPTER THREE

The bright rays of the sun
Bounce off the lilies of Hera
Yet the most beautiful sight
Is the sight of true love

THE FOLLOWING SUNDAY, both Smriti and Keshav's eagerness matched.

"Hi Keshav." Smriti nodded. She had added a hue to her lips.

"Hello, *Remembrance.*" Keshav smiled. He smelled of musk.

"And here goes my friend for two hours!" Mahesh grinned as Keshav and Smriti took seats beside each other. The cohort settled in around them, catching up and ordering their brunches – some ordering what they usually enjoyed and some with the mood to experiment.

The group played charades that day.

"Tuhina, you be in my team!" Mahesh nudged playfully.

"No way, I know you can't guess movies, let alone act!" Tuhina replied, batting her pink-lined eyes. "I'm with my girl, Usha." She joined Usha. Tuhina was wearing a sleeveless red-and-white checkered dress, and Usha was adorning a bottle-green-and-mustard ikkat saree. While Tuhina's eyes were lined with pink, Usha's were loaded with kohl.

"Hello, I would have been an actor if not a dentist, and I would have been fab and famous," Mahesh said. "Never mind, I'll team up with one of the boys."

"Wow! He's a dentist?" Smriti asked with surprise. Keshav nodded.

"Keshav?" Mahesh asked.

"No, I'm with Smriti," Keshav stated, turning toward her and asking, "is it okay?"

"Listen, I might be terrible," Smriti told him, "I haven't seen –"

"Make me lose, then," Keshav whispered. Smriti's face flushed red.

"I'll team up with you, Mahesh," Samir said.

The charades began. They stretched beyond their comfort zones to enact films. Smriti fortunately needed to enact for mere seconds before Keshav intuitively guessed the titles.

"These guys will win, hands down!" Samir said. "Come on Mahesh, buck up. Smriti and Keshav are ahead by three movies."

"We should split them up! They're a strong team," Juhi cried.

"I should have been paired up with Keshav. He is my boy. Smriti, give him back to me," Mahesh claimed.

"Fight for me Mahesh, fight for me!" Keshav joked along.

As the afternoon ended, Keshav gave in to the contemplation in his head.

"Will you hang out with me after this meeting today? There is something that I wish to do," Keshav asked her in a low voice. "It's been on my mind … I've been meaning to … umm … I was wondering if you'd help me," Keshav muttered muddled words under his breath.

I've to say no, it's all too fast, Smriti thought.

Smriti raised her eyebrows. "Too much has been happening since –"

"Orphanage," Keshav cut her short. "I have not been to one. And I'm dying to!" This lady would be the right one for his baby steps toward benevolence.

Smriti blinked. "Okay …" she said. "There is one I usually go to on our birthdays – mine and my daughter's, would you like to go there?"

"Please," Keshav said, enlivened.

After the group meet was over, Keshav and Smriti bought goodies for children and drove to the orphanage in Smriti's car.

The children knew Smriti and rushed to greet her. While Smriti chatted with them, Keshav filled their hands with toys, stationery, and chocolates.

Smriti comforted the children. "Which one of you hates washing socks … I can smell some roses?" She scrunched her nose. "Who was the detective in your game, and who was the *chor*?" "Who wants to become a doctor when they grow up, ah, an astronaut!" She taught them pranks. Keshav watched them from a distance, loving the intimate and humble rendezvous.

"Thank you for this opportunity!" Keshav beamed as he handed over the check to the matron. His need for altruism had found an outlet.

"And that ends our … day," Smriti said as they walked away from the institution.

"We still have our drive back," Keshav whispered.

"Were you always good with children?" Keshav asked, taking his seat in the car.

"Ever since I became a mother. Before that I knew nothing of children. But once I was a mom, I fell in love with kids. I always wanted my daughter's friends over." Smriti smiled, recalling the pre-school years when children from their apartment complex would gather in her house to eat mangoes. Recollecting memories, she put on her comfort music.

The notes filled the car, braiding their souls into one.

Keshav sang along.

"I am surprised you know of this ghazal. The singer is not that famous. Do you listen to similar music?" Smriti asked.

Keshav winked in response. "Just sing along!"

Smriti shook her head awkwardly.

"No, no …"

"Come on! I've heard you sing before … and I just saw you enact movie titles!"

Smriti blushed and sang along; her melodious voice deepened, drowning Keshav's dissonance.

She sings beautifully, Keshav thought. He glanced at her hand, not having the courage to hold it. Smriti heard him telepathically and reached out to his hand. She slipped her fingers into his, and blended her palm with his. Her earthiness was the perfect companion to the stirring waters of his core.

A comforting fuzziness originating from their guts melted their hearts.

From singing, they shifted to silence – the perfect setting to relish the warmth of their clasped palms and flushed cheeks.

***

Smriti searched around her closet, sieving through her holiday collection, and settled on a black tea-length dress. She put on makeup, not in the heavy manner girls did these days – she did not understand the products, with the bronzers, highlighters, and concealers – but in a traditional manner that smoothened her skin and highlighted her features.

Her phone buzzed.

Keshav? she thought before picking up the phone. *He must have reached. I've forgotten how to date.*

But it was Lata with her prompt:

"Dinner this weekend? Avantika is with grandparents, and Mohit has a meeting. So, we can chill at your place … if you don't want to go out!"

Smriti glanced at the message and gulped.

"We'll go out," her fingers penned each alphabet with the friendship-guilt.

"Woah! That's new!" came Lata's instant reply.

All my life's rules are bending ever since this man has come in, Smriti thought, *venting to people, singing in public, holding hands, dressing up in young-ish clothes, now going out at night …*

She viewed herself in the mirror. She hadn't worn a dress in years.

Wow, now before I decide to change, I should leave, she thought and rushed into her car, driving to their pre-decided dinner venue.

Keshav was already seated, dressed in an orange-collared T-shirt and jeans. His hair was pulled back with gel, making his forehead appear bigger, suiting his strong jawline and sharp features.

"You look beautiful," Keshav whispered, his twinkling eyes unable to concentrate on the food menu. "The dress suits you!"

"I bought it for my daughter's seventh birthday, eight years ago," Smriti confessed, ironing it with her palms. *I wish I could compliment him as easily,* Smriti thought, her scarlet cheeks giving away the depth to which his compliment had affected her.

"Oh, you fit into your old clothes. My Punjabi genes beat me there." Keshav grinned, picking up the menu. "And what is it that you'd like to eat, Smriti Jain? Jains are vegetarian … or is that one kind of Jain?"

"Yes, vegetarian," she confirmed. "What is new in the food menu?"

"The globalization in Indian restaurants is quicker with the advent of social media; we've dropped boundaries. Would you like a mezze platter?"

"Yes, sounds good. And no, both the Jains are vegetarian. Digambar and Svetambara … the main difference between the two beliefs is that of cladding – wearing clothes. In fact, some Digambara interpretations hold that women cannot achieve liberation and must be reborn as men to attain it!"

"Oh, why is that?" Keshav asked.

"They say that to achieve liberation, one has to adorn the sky, or *ambar*, as their clothing, and apparently women cannot do away with their clothes."

"Oh, interesting. Do you think of things like liberation?" he asked.

"*Haan thoda bahut* (Yes, a little bit). I hope I have paid my debts alongside, settled my karma. Do you believe in karma and its balancing?" Smriti asked.

"I do believe in karma and settling my sins within this life. I am a businessman, I understand the concept of time value. I don't want to atone with heavy interest loads," Keshav joked. Smriti smiled.

"Here, let's try the beer tasters. The servers have come by a few times now." Keshav handed a taster to Smriti.

She looked at the taster tray. When had she had beer before this? College?

She took one sip of it, and her face scrunched up.

Yuck, she thought, looking at Keshav for some motivation.

"This tastes like antibiotics, and this one tastes like a mushroom with fungus on top of it. I'll go for the Belgian one – it is fancy, but not very; you know how it is when you hit middle age – *calculated risks,*" he rallied along.

Smriti laughed and ordered the Belgian Witbier for herself too.

"While coming here I realized, I've done a lot at your beckoning. I never thought I'd open up like this again …"

"You're breaking self-imposed shackles, nothing else." A blush spread across his face. He met her eyes briefly and looked down at the table, fiddling with a paper napkin. "*Achha,* what is the quirkiest thing you do in your everyday life?"

"I shop the same things on Sunday and yet I make a fresh list for it every week," Smriti said in a low whisper.

"Quirky, Smriti, quirky. That's anything but quirky!"

She rolled her eyes and smiled. "Your turn."

"I need donuts during sad movies. I can't watch them without the support of sugar," Keshav admitted.

"That is cute!" Smriti smiled wide.

"What is your favorite movie?" Keshav asked, enjoying some cliché at his middle age.

"*Veer Zara.* That depth of love is unreal, and yet Shahrukh pulls it off! It amazes me. What about you? What's your favorite movie dialogue?"

Smriti asked in return, shaking away the goosebumps that *Veer Zara* brought onto her every single time!

"I used to watch *Harry Potter* a lot with my son, Kaveer, so after all this time –"

"Always!" Smriti completed the sentence.

They dug into their meal.

"The last time I went out for dinner was when my daughter was in town," Smriti shared.

"Where is she?" Keshav asked.

"In a boarding school in Indore …"

Smriti paused, and then continued, "In fact, Keshav, my daughter was talking about bullies in her letter. The sort of ragging she has mentioned is terrifying. I can't get my head over it," Smriti confessed.

"It is a part of boarding school life, though you should keep a check that she does not mess with them – these kids can get twisted. They don't know where to draw the line between fun and vindictiveness," Keshav replied.

"I fear sadists. They can go to any extent. Do you think I should bring her back?" Smriti asked in dismay.

"She has mentioned bullies, not that she is being bullied. These elements are everywhere in the society. You could teach her how to deal with them rather than running away. You can always bring her back if she is stressed. Besides, why did you send her to that school?"

"Umm … she began to sympathize with me. She felt responsible for my routine, cancelling plans with her friends to stay at home, feeling guilty about simple school trips. She wanted to be there for me. She should live her life, hang out with teenagers, and not adult quickly."

"It must have been a hard decision to make?"

"Actually, it wasn't. My colleagues had mentioned the school … I was skeptical at first but we decided to visit it. It was drizzling when we reached. Her curls, frizzier with the humidity, fell over her eyes but could not veil the admiration with which she viewed the infrastructure. I saw that she liked the place and didn't think twice before enrolling her," Smriti replied with nostalgia. "I know it is better for her future, but being away from each other hurts …"

"Bittersweet," Keshav stated. "Kaveer and I experience the same emotion. When we spend time together, we know it will end and he will have to go back to his mother. That energy looms throughout his trip."

"I can imagine …" Smriti said.

"Look at the time. It's 10:30! We didn't even need to play Jenga yet!"

"Good, because I would have taken time learning it!" Smriti said with a smile, removing the napkin from her lap and placing it on the table.

Keshav laughed and extended his hand across the table; she met it with hers. He caressed the top of her hand with his thumb. She blushed and beamed. The past fifteen years vanished from her life. For a while, she forgot that she was a woman who was living for her duties, her responsibilities. For those few hours, she lived to shake up a stony heart, to bring back lost vivacity, to caress her frigid soul. She set aside the mother in her and instead embraced the woman longing for affection.

His eyes met hers; her heart pounded against her chest. They ended the evening, longing with desire for one another.

While continuing her days of routine, Smriti relished a charm about herself. She studied herself in the mirror. Wrinkles were outlining her features; her body was that of a mother's – her breasts had drooped, her belly and hips bore fading scars from her pregnancy. She had overlooked her appearance for years, yet Keshav had found her beautiful. His eyes shone with honesty when he said it.

Looking at her reflection every day, she recalled his words and viewed herself through a lens of love. An awareness of her feminine energies made her feel alive.

Keshav experienced a similar flutter in the days that followed. What was it that drew him to Smriti? Was it her poise and simplicity? Was it the authentic smile that did not arise without enough reason? Was it the strength of a single mother that tugged at him? The stagnation in her soul was a prettier and more poignant poetry than love was.

He wanted to embrace that poetry, anchor his inner incompleteness into it.

***

When Lata saw Smriti enter the restaurant wearing jeans instead of her regular kurta set, her eyes widened and she nearly whistled.

"Is this really, Smriti … what is happening to you? It is the guy from the support group meeting, isn't it?"

Smriti blushed.

"Finally, what I've been trying to do for fifteen years, this man has done in a month! Our evening has to be about him! Tell me more!" Lata ventured, her voice piercingly loud and attention-seeking.

"Hush, you're so loud. We did meet. But details only after I speak with Jia about it. Till then, let's hear about film stars and your friends," Smriti said firmly.

"Not done ya! But I do have things to share. Do you know that actress, Yutika Khosla? She's been trying to lead a Malayalam film – she almost got her big break, she worked on the script of the film, except her cousin rolled in and scooped the pie! They chose her over Yutika for the lead! God knows what happened behind closed doors, but the row between them is out in public. I'm again on damage control."

"Gosh, cousins stealing business is still happening in the world!" Smriti grinned, listening to Lata go on. "I used to watch that in serials."

"It has gotten worse. People aren't satisfied with their own lives. As a result, they either want other people to fail, or they live dual lives. If they're having a perfect career, they're shadowing it with drugs; if they have a perfect marriage, they're shadowing it with an affair. And this desire for masala in life is unending and ruinous. Not like I should complain, masala is my bread and butter …"

"Well, they could be getting things easy! In the eighties and the nineties, love and friendship were hard to find, careers took time to be built … Ask me! I am easily satisfied with whatever life has to offer!"

Lata stopped talking and gazed at the table before her in a daze. She stared and fiddled with her margarita glass. She twirled the stem of the glass in her fingers, spilling some of the drink on the table.

"Lata – do you have something to share?" Smriti said, reading between the lines.

Lata tugged at her shirt dress and sipped her drink. She studied her surroundings, then admitted to Smriti in a whisper, "It is nothing. I think I figure in the unsatisfied strata. Don't know how you've been doing it. Home to work, work to home. Shouldering responsibilities, I get tired with the rut of life …"

"But –" Smriti raised her eyebrows in alarm, but Lata clarified, "No, I promise, there is no one else. I love Mohit. I wouldn't tip-toe any lines. But I get exhausted. Emotionally, mentally, physically. And he's hardly available for me or Avantika. He is barely home. And he has these superwoman expectations from me …"

"Then talk to him about it. These shadows are not the solution. You have the perfect home. In fact, if I ever had to drop Jia and travel, it would be at your home! So please take a holiday, read interesting books, quit your job, jump off a cliff, but don't hurt your home to fill up your emptiness."

Everyone in my support group would kill for her family life, Smriti thought.

"I know, right. I am blessed. Remind me to see it. I should talk to Mohit – I don't know how, I don't want to sound needy. Men simply don't realize things on their own, do they?!" Lata expressed.

"Not experienced enough to comment, sorry!" Smriti said.

"On another note, I'm making Avantika meet a nutritionist."

"*Hey Bhagwan*! (Oh God!) Avantika is TEN! Lata …" Smriti said, stunned. "You're paranoid over nothing! Please let her eat, Lata!"

"It is only regulated meals …" Lata rolled her eyes.

Smriti laughed along. "You've always been crazy! Please don't do that, or else of course she's going to talk about body shaming."

"Ya, okay stop giving me the spouse and mommy guilts!" Lata rolled her eyes, finishing her margarita and ordering another one.

***

Smriti and Keshav met again mid-week. Mumbai's skyline was painted with shades of the setting sun, a marbled orange, pink, and purple. The skyscraper lights were timidly illuminating the sky; the stars were visible to those with the sharpest eye-sight. The sounds of the birds, invisible to the eyes, were battling to be heard over the honks of the cars.

They walked along the Marine Drive promenade. A gentle breeze rising from the expansive sea welcomed them with its dewy scent. The horizon stretched ahead of them, basking in the sun's final embrace.

As they sat by the boulevard, Smriti filled Keshav's hand with hers. The fit pulsed with a strong sense of belongingness.

"No matter the age, a pretty sky is what lights one up," Smriti said in a hushed voice, gazing at that half of the sky that was tinted with twilight.

"What one seeks is the same at any age, Smriti …"

"But we learn to cope without getting what we once desired. Haven't we become survivors?"

"Yes, we have. But it makes life simple, you know. We know how our decisions have turned out. We have to accept things the way they are and relish whatever life has to offer now …" Keshav said.

"I've not regretted having my kid," Smriti stated straight forwardly.

"I did not mean that," Keshav replied light-heartedly, before adding, "I was saying it from my point of view, in fact. Time and again, I've regretted my divorce since I lost my son to it. I haven't taken it as bravely as I assumed I would. But putting him through a custody fight never made sense."

"Tell me about him ..." Smriti nudged on.

"Hmm. He is a generous kid. Very loving. He held us together when we lost Lily. That made him mature early. Our evening routine was my favorite. After dinner, we would spend hours over Lego while our strained eyes fought for sleep. We shifted from film numbers to *kirtan* before we dozed off, me quicker than him!" Keshav sounded desolate. "He was my partner-in-crime for the donut-binging during movies. Funnily, I cried quicker than my baby boy. I still recall his sweet voice telling me, 'What Papa, superheroes don't cry!' I was his superhero." His eyes swelled as he spoke. "You know what, the glory that we give to true love, belongs to parenthood. Truest romantic love, cannot fill a child's shoe."

Smriti side-hugged him. They gazed into the horizon together.

"How old is your daughter?"

"She is fifteen."

"What kind of a person was her father, and how did you meet him?"

"I met him at an interview immediately after college. We were contending for the same job. I remember bickering about our chances. For the three years that followed, we were inseparable. Until, of course, I trusted him, and he broke it."

"Ever since, have you been managing her by yourself?" Keshav had done everything he could for Kaveer even though his marriage had not worked out.

"He is married elsewhere," Smriti replied.

"Please tell me you got that job! Over him I mean?" He smirked caringly.

"Ha ha, I did! I was an achiever back then. You wouldn't have recognized me from college! I was exceptional at extra-curriculars and popular!" Smriti claimed.

"You're right, I can't imagine you being a popular girl. Motherhood changes women. I noticed that with my ex-wife. On that topic, I still don't know your daughter's name!" Keshav said.

"I have maintained that purposely. I want to keep her life private. Maybe once she is comfortable with our equation ..." Smriti replied.

Keshav pulled her closer to him. She rested her head on his chest and nestled inward. The outlandish arm around her made her feel a rare security. Someone wanted to listen to her, spend time with her, and pierce her inherent stillness.

"My daughter's name was Lily. My late mother kept the name. Lily was with us for two years, and a simple fever took her," he shared, without Smriti's probing. "She resembled Neha. In fact, both the children took after her. Lily was peaceful; after bringing up a naughty Kaveer, she was this happy doll in our lives. She cried little and seldom kept us up at night … One night, she got fever, we took her to the doctor, and I distinctly remember, he prescribed paracetamol. She left us that night. There was no reason for her to leave us yaar …"

A rawness filled his throat and chest. He had put away those memories in a box to be a harbor for his wife and son, but his stoic endeavors had buried the ache instead of resolving it. He could not look at Smriti, so he watched the sea waves instead.

She grazed his wet cheek with her palm.

"Even though Neha was the one who carried the children, I was a natural father. I miss being a parent, Smriti. I miss bringing him up. I don't want to see him on holidays, borrowing him like he is not mine. I am not a stranger. I'm a father, and I long to be a father again," Keshav continued.

"I'm so sorry. Life can be absurd. I'm a single mother without a partner, and you're a parent living with the memory of your children." Smriti stroked his hand. She sunk into his tender torso.

She concentrated on two things – his heartbeat and the sound of waves hitting the rocks, a magnificent symphony for her. She no longer wanted to talk about what had gone wrong, because for once in her life, she was where she belonged.

"When do you go back to Singapore?" Smriti asked with a heavy heart.

"Three weeks," Keshav stated solemnly.

Smriti glanced at him, acknowledging that the rules she had lived life with were broken. She was attached, her guard was down, and she wanted to tell Jia about him.

CHAPTER FOUR

As we tip toe through slender paths
Duty is the rope we hold on to
While the heart is the torch
The soul is the soldier that marches on

"NO MUMMA, THERE is nothing eventful at school," Jia said in a blunt tone.

"Did Srishti's parents pull her out or has any action been taken against the bullies?" Smriti asked.

"No, she hasn't told her parents yet," Jia said.

"She should inform them. Achha, tell me about your inter-houses?" Smriti asked, covering up.

"*Dance and debate ka chal raha hai* (Dance and debate are going on). I'm not participating in any of them. Too outgoing for me. I might get the pottery prize for the year from my batch. I made a five feet tall mold pot! The teacher was impressed so she's nominated me for the prize. Teacher *bhi interesting hai* (teacher is also interesting), she previously taught at Rabindranath Tagore's school – Shantiniketan! *Unse baat karke achha lagta hai* … (I like speaking with her…)"

"Array even I did pottery! Remember that support group I told you about? One Sunday we made sushi together and the previous Sunday we had a pottery session!"

"Wow Mom, *sushi banaya aapne* (you made sushi?)! And pottery was fun, right?" Jia said.

Smriti recalled their pottery session. Smriti and Keshav had made tiny clay sculptures – the Merlion from Singapore, the Gateway of India from Mumbai, a heart, a boat. They made the heart sit on the boat and sail from the Merlion to Gateway of India, like teenagers in love.

Smriti took the Merlion back as a keepsake and Keshav pocketed the Gateway of India. Smriti placed it in her living room, next to framed pictures of Jia and herself. Keshav placed it in his laptop bag as a good luck charm.

Smriti wanted to tell her about Keshav, but it was a conversation to be held face to face!

"*Padhai kaisi chal rahi hai?* (How are studies going on?) You should start thinking about your subjects in Class Eleven now. *Art toh aap additional le sakte ho* (Art can be an additional subject)… but between Commerce, Humanities, and Science …"

"Studies are average. I haven't fared well. *Aayegi aapko report card. Mann nahi karta padhai karne ka* (You'll get the report card. I don't feel like studying …" Jia's voice was husky.

"But why beta? You told me you liked mathematics, geography … at least score well in the subjects you like … You were performing so well in your school here …"

"Mummy, I've got to go. The matron is saying time is up …" Her volume simmered low.

"*Ek minute* (Just a minute), are you eating well?"

"*Haan theek hai sab* (Yes, everything is fine), bye *ab*!!" Jia said swiftly.

"Mumma sends you hugs." Smriti's eyes brimmed.

"I love you, *beti*," she added, fidgeting with the newspaper in her hands. She had torn the edges into small bits.

***

All Keshav had told Smriti was that they were going somewhere formal.

She readied herself in a white, sleeveless dress. She styled her hair differently. She applied a rare ruddy lip color to finish her look.

The clock struck 8; her doorbell rang. She opened the door to find him standing before her, dressed in a tux and a tie. Though he usually bore charming looks, that evening he looked sexy. The tux brought out his broad shoulders and height.

Smriti's skin tingled. DeSire swam through her veins. She wanted to kiss him. She wanted to slant her head, avoid their noses, submerge in a movie-like kiss that was vehement enough to blank her mind.

"Are you going to keep staring at me? Invite me inside?" Keshav chuckled. He acted confident while his heart somersaulted.

"Inside? Are we having our date in my house?" Smriti was puzzled. She glanced around – not a cushion was out of place.

"No, but we have fifteen minutes to kill," Keshav announced.

"For what?" Smriti asked, bewildered.

Hovering over her, he placed a hand on her waist, and tugged her close to himself. He placed his lips on her peeking shoulders. Shivers ran through her body. Goosebumps awakened her.

She let out a giggle. "I'm sorry, I haven't done this in a while. And where are we going? You've got me anxious and turned on, both. I can't take so much!"

"We are going for a salsa class, *Remembrance,*" he announced, turning her around, placing a kiss on her forehead, still keeping her close to him.

"Salsa? From where do you come up with these ideas? Sorry to break it to you, I don't dance … I was born with two absolute left feet!" Smriti stated worriedly. "If you see me dance, you'd run for your life."

"*Oho* … I am going to lead, and it is a class, not a stage performance," Keshav convinced her.

"Will there be more people?" Smriti asked.

"No. I arranged a private class!" Keshav said, grinning.

Their faces were inches away, sharing a gaze.

A string of energy pulled Keshav into Smriti. He dived deep into her core. Slowly, he planted a tender kiss on her parted lips. Her lips trembled with desire. The moment's silence engulfed them and immersed them in the shared affection.

Too overwhelmed to keep her in his arms any longer, Keshav broke the eye contact. "Come, let's go."

"Yeah. This was … too much." Her mind, body, and soul throbbed with affection and electricity.

As they danced together, the intimacy between them grew, and their breaths converged with one another's. Their bodies dipped to the rhythm of classical numbers. After every few steps, they paused to laugh at Smriti's lack of rhythm.

"After I go back, she's going to continue with dance classes here," Keshav told the dance teacher after their session.

"I'm sorry, he's joking," Smriti said, holding his arm and leaning into him.

"No, you really need to practice." Keshav laughed.

"I'll practice dancing, you will practice making sushi, deal?" Smriti said.

"Done deal!" Keshav promised.

"When we meet next, I'll do salsa with you and you make sushi for me," Smriti said.

After the dance class, Smriti invited Keshav over to her apartment. His stay in Mumbai was coming to an end. Smriti no longer wanted to stop herself from falling madly in love with him. She did not know where it would go, or how Jia would feel about it. But for once in her life, she wanted to feel his touch on her body. She wanted to be swayed by the melodious breeze he had brought into her life.

The moment they hit the door of the apartment, they were washed with streams of passion.

He first looked into her eyes and then shut his to soak her energy in. His lips touched hers and swayed them. Her plump sumptuous lips delved back into his mouth, embracing their candid throbbing hearts, setting forth a connection that was bestowed with magnificence.

With their lips locked, he placed his hand on her waist. He stroked it tenderly upward, reaching the base of her breasts. She let out a moan as he cupped her. She undressed herself. His mouth followed his hands, he kissed her navel, her breasts, and the nape of her neck. He traced the center of her breasts with his fingers, gearing her racing heart and arousing her.

Then suddenly, she cut the moment off. The conformist mother in her won. She closed her eyes and apologized to him. Her life was not hers alone.

"Sorry," she whispered, meeting his eye with guilt.

"No, it's alright." He took her in an embrace.

She dug her head in his chest. She breathed out her ardor, realizing that though she had stopped herself from going all the way, she was alive now. Her life was no longer a vehicle of duty alone – it was going to crave and urge. She was going to experience joy and pain with a higher intensity. She was going to feel love, and she was even going to feel heartbreak. In that moment of passion, light had entered her.

And he was the one who had connected her with her spirit.

A teardrop left her eye. He wiped it away with kisses. He smooched her face with devotion.

"Stay over," Smriti whispered, tracing his face with her finger.

He nodded. They moved to the bed, and listening to a song, they slept off.

The next morning, Keshav woke up earlier than Smriti and headed out to the living room.

He observed the pictures that were placed together in the living room. They were centered around Smriti's daughter. Her nose was like Smriti's, sharp, and her eyes, though of a different color, hazel, had the same depth. Apart from her nose, nothing was Smriti's – she had curly hair and rosy cheeks, the exact kind the nursery rhyme "Chubby cheeks" was based on.

There was one picture in which she was a toddler and she was playing with balloons; one in which she was on stage, receiving an award in school; a couple of her solo pictures from varied stages of life; and there was one with the both of them, from when she was about eight or nine. That was the oldest picture there was.

He picked the one with Smriti and her daughter in it. They were the perfect picture of love. There was a hint of sacrifice and unwavering, unconditional affection in Smriti's eyes.

He fidgeted with the picture he held in his hand.

She is taken, he thought to himself. She was committed to somebody. While dating a mother, he was stepping into something that was deep and sacred. For a split second, he wanted to embrace them as his family.

Smriti entered the living room and hugged him from the back.

"Oh, you've seen what my love looks like then …" Smriti announced, smiling.

"Come here." He signaled her to hug him. She drowned into his torso and clutched him tight. "It must be even harder for you to be living for her but without her company."

"How have you opened up to me?" he added with astonishment, playing with her hair and kissing her head.

"Thank you for coming my way. I did not even know how terribly I needed this," Smriti submitted.

Keshav gazed into her glinting eyes and understood the kind of trust she placed in him.

***

Samir had planned a day's excursion for the support group. It entailed traveling to a particular spot for a trek. Eleven kilometers from Lonavala, the Lohagarh Fort trek was a beautiful walk.

Smriti was not the sporty kind.

"Good morning, I'm anxious about the trek," she texted Keshav upon waking up.

Keshav was putting on a cap. He placed the cap in different directions – forward, backward, and sideways.

Am I too old to pull off a backward? he deliberated, turning it forward and tucking in his T-shirt in his cargo shorts.

"Morning, it's a nature walk … Besides, I will be holding your hand," he replied, reading Smriti's message.

Smriti smiled. While sipping her lemongrass tea, she set a reminder to call Jia at the scheduled time. She fetched out her old sneakers, dusted them, and put them on with her kurta.

Before leaving the house, she glanced at the mirror.

So strange these shoes look on me … she thought.

The support group gathered for the mini-bus ride to Lonavala. Keshav and Smriti immediately took their seats together. Keshav gave Smriti a peck on her cheek once they sat down on their seats. Smriti took his hand in hers.

"I like your cap," Smriti said.

"You wear it," Keshav replied. He took it off and put it over her head.

The drive from Mumbai to Lonavala was picturesque. The morning sun's rays bounced off the green hills. Waterfalls of different heights transcended into autumn mists and manifested into low-lying clouds. These misty clouds swam through the windows of the bus, appearing heavenly.

"*Bore ho rahe hai* (We're getting bored), let's sing songs," Seema said.

"Yes, songs!" Juhi clamored along.

"Guys, Yuvraj will be leaving the support group as he is no longer single! It is his last day with us," Samir announced.

"Let him start singing then," Tuhina said.

"Okay, cool … let me dedicate something to all of you … *tere jaisa yaar kahaan … kahaan aisa yaarana …*"

Seema picked the next song. "I'm dedicating this to the weather today … *Rhim jhim gire saawan …*"

Keshav sang one of Smriti's favorite ghazals:

"Ab kya ghazal sunau … Tumhe dekhne k baad …"

"Array humaare Talat Aziz!" Mahesh jeered.

"Mahesh, tell me something about Keshav from his school time," Smriti asked.

"Keshav Chopra. He had a crush on this girl, Rashmeet. Probably because she was the only other Punjabi in class. But they had never spoken to each other and she asked him for his exam sheet to cheat from. He got caught passing it to her. The teacher beat him up! Was it pre-boards, Keshav?"

"Yeah, pre-boards. Thank God it wasn't boards. I would have had to skip a year!" Keshav added, "Rashmeet didn't even thank me!"

"Man, the things this man does in love … Smriti, my friend is a real *heera* (diamond)," Mahesh added.

The group laughed.

"On that note, our *Talat Aziz* will sing us another song," Samir added.

They reached Lonavala and headed for their trek.

The vibrant green trees rustled lightly with the fresh breeze that blew that day. Bunches of tiny wildflowers created pockets of wonder as the morning sun embraced them.

The group reached the top of the Lohagarh Fort and rested.

For this group, who lived a life of routine and got little time to explore nature, the white misty haze that simmered at eye level flushed them with tranquility.

Some of them sat in silence, admiring the views that lay ahead of them. Some of them placed earphones in their ears to enjoy the music they did not get time for otherwise. While another lot, used the trek as another topic to jeer and cheer over.

"Mahesh is all talk; he was the slowest amongst the lot. He was even behind me!" joked Tuhina.

"Tuhina, you do realize you were about to slip twice and I saved your life because I was behind you? You should be grateful to me; I am the God that granted you a second life," Mahesh teased her back, relishing the one-up.

After resting with the group and laughing at Mahesh's constant chatter, Keshav and Smriti walked through the fort, observing the ruins together. They found a small deserted temple under one of the caves. A stone *Shivalinga* was placed in a square abyss.

Smriti kneeled by the Shivalinga, closed her eyes, and prayed. Keshav watched from a distance. She walked back to Keshav, and they sat at a distance from the group.

Keshav remarked, "You are a believer, aren't you?"

Smriti replied, "I am; the kind to pray and not question. How about you?"

Keshav replied, "I am agnostic. At one point I was an atheist."

"Really?" Smriti asked.

"Yes."

"How did you go from being an atheist to agnostic?"

"For the longest time I did not understand the concept of God. My logical brain didn't accept religion. But over time I realized, if you don't have faith, you can't find God. I understood that I could be blocking God's presence. My lack of faith being overthrown was brilliant. Agnostic now … almost a believer!"

"My daughter is not a believer."

"Maybe someday when I meet your daughter I will shift her from being an atheist to becoming a questioner too."

"Does one believe after questions are answered? I haven't questioned faith."

"Exactly. It is why you perceive God. Because you are open to it. No questions are entirely answered. Most answers are paradoxes. So those paradoxes are not going to satisfy us anyway. It is the journey that matters. Questioning creates space for newer things, growth, and beauty. So questioning is what is important. If your daughter learns to question, she will find it more enriching than believing or non-believing."

Smriti watched the views ahead of her.

"What makes you happy?" Keshav continued the conversation.

"These days it's been you!" Smriti replied, pinching him on his arm.

Keshav asked, "What makes you unhappy?"

Smriti answered, "Well, even though my life isn't entirely 'lively', death makes me sad."

Closing her eyes, she took a deep breath in.

"There is something about being here, breathing, that feels safe, and somehow the end of it feels unsettling. Doesn't death give the feeling that the journey was futile? The fact that it has to end, reduces the intensity of life… Perhaps, on some level it is why I believe in God. To bring in a sensation of eternity…"

"Journeys don't end with death, they transform … Only gross matter returns to dust, the subtle, the spirit, lives on … So don't be sad about death, *Remembrance* … you're eternal …"

She took off the cap and put it on Keshav's head. Keshav tidied Smriti's hair, pushing a lock behind her ear and settling the few strands that had gotten untidy because of the cap.

At 11:00 a.m., Smriti's alarm reminder rang to call Jia up. But there was no network on her phone. She restarted her phone, still no network. She borrowed phones from the group.

"Does anybody have network on their phone?" Keshav asked the group.

Everyone said no.

Smriti exchanged a worried look with Keshav.

"She'll be waiting for my call," Smriti told Keshav, troubled.

"Can you call her once you're back?" Keshav asked sympathetically.

"No, they have strict call timings," Smriti replied.

"Call her teacher and leave a message," Keshav replied.

"There isn't another option anyway," Smriti said.

Soon the time to call Jia slipped by.

For the remainder of the day, her mind was with Jia. When she did get network, she called Jia's matron to convey her apology.

"Sure. I will let her know," the matron replied.

That reduced the burden. Still, she had never missed a call.

***

"Yes, their tech is strong. I can vouch for it. In fact, they will be applying for a patent as soon as they get an investment. They need someone to market it for them from there on," Keshav said on his phone.

Mahesh was standing at the other edge of Keshav's office, waiting for him to hang up, making paper planes while he waited. He threw a plane at Keshav.

"If the investor has a network to assist them with their market reach, he can get more equity," Keshav said, hanging up and chuckling as the plane hit him.

"You're not fit to come to office, Mahesh," Keshav said to him, grinning, taking the plane in his hands.

"You're the one who wanted to meet at office. I told you let's go out. Stinky workaholic," Mahesh jested. "You're working all the time, and the little time you have left, you're spending with Smriti. Man, I shouldn't have introduced you to her. It is so irritating."

"What? You should be happy for me!" Keshav expressed.

"Why? You forget, you're not the only single one, I'm divorced too!" Mahesh said.

"I'm sorry," Keshav apologized. "Let's find you someone!"

"I can't do anything until my divorce case is closed. But once that happens, ladies will have to watch out for me. I'm excited to date again! I am sure I will find someone as soon as I am legally single," Mahesh said.

"As if it is that easy!" Keshav retorted.

"It will be for me. Anyway, what happened to your 'Any company I provide would be fleeting'? What about the two of you when you go to Singapore?"

"I wish I could take her with me. Or move in here with her. I don't mind either. This director I worked with two months back has offered me a pretty good deal."

"You're talking gibberish. Her kid is a teenager. You've fallen in love without meeting her kid. It will be super complicated. I'm a father too. I can't imagine my kids adapting to another man," Mahesh stated.

"But that kid has never had a father," Keshav said. "She might warm up to me?"

"As always, Keshav finds a silver lining! Let's hope she likes you, otherwise you'll have ignored your friend for a fling. Not worth it!"

Keshav laughed. "I'm sorry. Tell me, how can I entertain you?"

"Just pour me a drink," Mahesh said irritably.

***

"May I?" He placed his right hand behind her neck, making her skin tingle. He delved into her mouth, parting her lips with his. Smriti broke the intimate lip lock to suck his chin. Keshav traced her right side with his index finger.

"Come, I'll take you to the terrace of the building," Smriti interrupted the moment, in an ardor-filled whisper. Her eyes twinkled as she held his hand and led him upstairs. Evening shades filled the sky. It was dark, but not daunting; it was lit with street-lights rather than stars. They could hear a *baraat* from afar.

Smriti sat on a cemented bench and tugged at Keshav's arm. "Sit here."

"Hey, look at that cloud. It is beautifully lit up," Keshav wondered out loud, his heart still throbbing from the kiss.

"It is because the moon is hiding behind it, silly." Smriti understood the sky better than anyone. It was her companion during her lonely nights. When Jia was a baby and she found it difficult to raise her alone, she came up to the terrace and watched the stars. The cosmos was as much hers as anyone else's … Unlike love, it was not partial.

"It is glistening with satisfaction that it is the sole cloud being entrusted with the secrets of the moon for the night," Keshav said loudly, breaking Smriti's reminiscence.

"Wow that is … artistic!" Smriti smiled at Keshav's imagination.

"I am talented, aren't I?" Keshav giggled again.

Smriti laughed and quietly prayed to the stars. *"Please capture this moment and remind me when I need company. Please store this joy for me. I want this moment to last forever …"*

Keshav studied her face; it was like the cloud that was camouflaging the moon – her face was covering her beautiful endless soul. He had understood her, like a piece of art. He wanted to keep this piece of art forever – he wanted to make it his constant home. He wanted to live with it.

"I wonder why this has happened now. You know, your entering my life," Smriti said.

"Well, what matters is what you want to do about it. Would you like to move with me to Singapore?" Keshav asked.

"It is early to talk about that," Smriti replied.

"But maybe it is not?" Keshav convinced her. "Is it our age to play games? It's our age to dive deep into it."

"But can we do long distance and see where it goes?" Smriti suggested.

"That's leaving a lot to chance. I don't trust chance."

"We'll know if we are meant to be together …"

"We are meant to be together," Keshav said and sat down on his knee.

"Stop kidding me, get up, Keshav!" Smriti beamed, exhilarated. "I cannot believe this."

"Smriti, will you –" Keshav's starry eyes made it her brightest night.

"Listen, once I've spoken to her and she goes back to school, I will plan my leaves and come meet you!" Smriti sputtered. "You're crazy cute."

"You don't want to be with me?" Keshav asked.

"Of course I do! I'm not saying no at all. I'm saying, we have to wait! I need to speak with my kid. She has to approve of us," Smriti said, giggling.

She cupped his face in her palms, drew him inward, and kissed him deeply. His supple lips tugged at her stagnation. They whispered to her core, that the universe loved her.

***

"Are you home?" Lata texted Smriti on Tuesday evening.

Another text followed: *"I'm coming."*

Smriti paced her living room.

Suddenly, a lot is going on in my life, she thought.

Lata pushed the apartment door open and hugged Smriti.

She was crying. "Avantika doesn't want to come home. She says we aren't there for her. Complaining about me to her grandmother – that I don't let her eat, I work Sundays, blah blah. She says she'll stay with her *dadi.* She's been asking them to top up her pocket money so she can shop bigger brands. Smriti, help me!"

"Don't cry! What does Mohit say?" Smriti asked.

"He says it's not easy to live with his mom. She'll come running back home in a week!" Lata replied, wiping her tears, "But it is not that. My daughter doesn't want to live with me! How terrible a mother am I?"

"Everything will be okay … sit down," Smriti said, heading to the kitchen to bring her a drink.

"Fresh lime?" Smriti asked.

"Add some vodka to it, please," Lata replied.

"Sit, Lata ..." Smriti motioned her to the sofa.

"There are two more years for her to become a teenager, why has this begun early? She's already rebelling."

"It's normal ... don't worry please," Smriti said. "You should reduce your working hours if Avantika feels strongly about it. And about her meals, let time sort that out. She'll know what is good for her and what is not, as time passes. She'll want to be healthy."

"I hope so, Smriti! Was Jia a difficult kid?" Lata asked.

Smriti gulped and thought, *she was the easiest kid there ever was.*

"She had her days ..." Smriti hugged Lata.

"I know that Mohit and I have prioritized our careers, but why does it have to be a deal? We enjoy working ... doesn't mean we're bad parents. I'm unable to track what she is learning from which friend of hers," Lata confided. "Imagine complaining about me to my mother-in-law!"

"Relax! Maybe she misses a sibling ..." Smriti said.

"It is possible. It could be a common problem with small families ... Why don't Jia and you come over for Diwali? Avantika and Jia can bond," Lata said.

"Okay, we will come by. Yes, Avantika and Jia can spend time together. Don't fret. And both of you spend time at home. Spending time with Mohit might reduce your dissatisfaction with life ..."

Lata stuck her tongue out.

***

Smriti woke up on Wednesday to her newspaper and fortnightly letter from Jia.

`Hello Mummy,`

`Hope you are doing well.`

`I got my first period - it was bad, Mummy. I was in pain, could not get out of bed. The teachers were indifferent because by now everyone in the dorm has gotten it. I was the last in my dorm. They got it when they were 12 or 13. I am terrified of the time` of the month now. Girls have to go through loads, boys are lucky.

Our art inter-house is next week - I am representing the house in the cartooning competition - making Roger Federer's cartoon sketch!

Our house has lost in swimming inter-house. Somehow, we are bad in sports.

Anya's parents had come and they got us loads of chocolates to binge on. The house mistress was a deal to convince to let us keep them.

Srishti is still having a hard time with the bullies. They have asked the class not to talk to her. She is my friend, how do I not talk to her? Anyone who complains about them to the teachers gets bullied by the seniors as well.

Nevertheless, apart from that, everything is alright. We play games in the dorm - Mishika and I played catch with a ball for three continuous hours without dropping it. Anya sneaked in cards to play with.

I miss your cooking. I miss you, Mummy, and our Wednesday night spaghetti and pizzas.

Diwali holidays are from the 15th of October for four days. Looking forward to seeing you.

Love,

Jia

As Smriti folded the letter, she cried. The letter was typed before Sunday, and she had missed calling Jia amidst her period. She cringed as she reread the letter, getting angry at herself. She took out her stationery instantly and sketched out strength for Jia.

Jia,

My heart.

Heartiest congratulations on your period. I understand your pain and I send you sooooo many hugs for it; but you are now a grown girl!!! I am happy for you. I remember the day I got you home from the hospital - a tiny little bundle, with tiny fingers, grasping my fingertip - you were a sight of wonder. I had never owned a jewel as precious, let alone adorned her in my arms … and today you have touched your menarche! I wish I was there to see you blossom and succeed in bearing your menstruation.

Also, I agree, my child, that a woman's journey is not an easy one. Physically, women do have to bear a lot, and that strength adds to the beauty of a woman. We women are formidable, my baby. When you come for Diwali, remind me, together we will study about Indian mythology and the goddesses.

Do carry that cartooning sketch back with you, we will frame it and hang it on our living room wall.

I am sorry, my child, that I missed calling on Sunday. I was in a no-network zone. I hope you can forgive your Mummy this once for slipping.

About the bullying, as a mother, I worry for your benefit, but I would not tell you to abandon your friend. Remember, you can help someone else if you are in a good position yourself. The better way to go about it is to get on a good page with everyone and then politely suggest that there is no reason to bully or demean others.

I am going to speed-post this letter. I hope everything else is well.

Love always,

Mummy

CHAPTER FIVE

Matrescence,
As pure as the river stream
That flows from heaven
The memory of the chord
Is the strongest of manifestations

THEY STOOD OUTSIDE the airport, prolonging their goodbyes. Keshav's graying roots had lengthened, the crease at the corner of his eyes had softened, but his brow was stiff with worry.

A rendezvous that had shaken their souls, given them energy to live on, was coming to an end.

"Will you come to Singapore soon?" Keshav asked, his eyes acknowledging the sadness in his heart.

She nodded. He played with her fingers to soothe his anxiety.

"Will you tell your daughter – I still don't know her name – about me?"

"I will," she replied.

Smriti did not want it to be an emotional goodbye. She wanted to be stronger, but something made her insecure. *Was she parting ways with him forever?* Her heart skipped a beat; tears brimmed up. Those brimming tears turned into unexpected blubber. She was saying goodbye to the person who had accepted her the way she was, taken her around her city, made her step out of her comfort zone, cared for her, kissed her, and shown her that she was important to the universe. He had awakened her, made her smile amidst a life of responsibility, made her skin tingle, and set her mellow desires on fire.

They held hands, intertwining fingers in a wishful manner, hoping that they would meet soon.

Keshav pulled her into a long hug. They both wanted to say that they loved each other, to commit their emotions into a tangible existence, but they drowned their voices deeper within themselves. They communicated it through their eyes, through the touch of their hands.

"Do you ever think of coloring your hair?" he asked, breaking the emotional silence and kissing her on her head.

"No. Why, do you not like it?" Smriti asked, looking up from his chest to his face. The smell of his aftershave was familiar.

"I love it. Your salt-and-pepper … and your no-piercing ears!" Keshav pulled her closer to him.

"Remember our deal: you'll learn how to make sushi, and I'll learn how to dance," Smriti said.

"Yes. Promise. Our first dinner together, I'll cook for you. And for your daughter also," Keshav said.

"I'll go now. You take care of yourself, laugh more!" he murmured, pulling away.

Keshav turned on his heel and left through the departure entrance. When he had come to India, he had been a lonely, incomplete man, Smriti's simplicity had completed him.

His mind sifted through their previous night. The easy kiss she had planted on his ears, the sensation of his lips on her hair, the trace of her fingertips on his chest – the dive into one another's depths. The tight hug she had given in the middle of the night, kicking off her blanket and entering his. Their body scents had merged into one. His lips tingled with the memory of its mate …

His heart was at its troughs – it would be desolate in his empty penthouse. He turned back. Smriti had left.

He had left their beautiful bond exposed to the fickle plans of the universe.

He checked the phone number he had – yes, she was a call away.

"*Boarded*," he texted her, setting forth a long-distance relationship.

Smriti, back home, was continuing with her routine, when her phone buzzed with his message and she smiled. "Oh, thank God for this silly phone …"

She opened the letter Jia had sent her and re-read it. They had not spoken in twelve days, the longest ever. Jia had had her first period without her around.

Jia would have felt terrible, Smriti thought. *I hope they gave her the message. What if she worries about me?*

After the period sentence was something happy, and then there was something about bullying again. Her heart skipped a beat. There were two major things written in the letter.

Though it was not her fault that she couldn't reach Jia the previous Sunday, guilt hung within her.

She went for a walk on the terrace at night and video-called Keshav.

It is a new moon day, she thought, looking for the moon.

He showed her his place, a penthouse overlooking other high-rises of Singapore, dazzling with lights.

"Fancy, *haan*," Smriti joked.

"Yes, but empty," Keshav replied.

He told her about his start-ups.

"I want to do something meaningful," Keshav said. "I need to build better entrepreneurs; ideas are nothing by themselves."

"Why don't you open up a business school, or have a program for budding entrepreneurs?" Smriti said.

"I like the idea, but there is more theory than hands-on practice of handling businesses in schools. Organizing short programs maybe … I will think about it," Keshav thought out aloud.

"I am thinking of enrolling for some hobbies. Dancing lessons for sure. But I want to paint. Tuhina knew of a painting teacher," Smriti said. "By the way, have you had dinner?"

"I picked up a sandwich while exiting the airport … I have a Sri Lankan didi who comes and makes my dinners here. She'll resume from tomorrow. Lunches are usually in office or on the go," Keshav explained.

"I could have packed some Indian food for you," Smriti offered. She went down from the terrace to her apartment.

"Come stay with me," he said.

"Someday," Smriti replied.

"Do you want to crash together on video call?" Keshav asked.

"Yes." Smriti nodded, taking him to the bedroom with her.

They both slept looking at one another.

***

It was on the fourth call that Smriti picked up.

"Hello, is that Ms Smriti Jain?" a woman said in a grave voice.

"Yes." Smriti was groggy. *But a call at…* she checked the time – *3:30 a.m.*

This call. The time. A woman on the other side.

Her maternal heart shook from its place.

"Jia? Is Jia, okay?" Smriti's asked in a quivering voice, bewildered.

"This is her teacher from school. You need to rush to Indore, Ma'am, unfortunately there has been an accident." The voice was blunt yet sympathetic.

"Accident?" Smriti yelled, filled with horror and panic.

"She tried to die by suicide, Ma'am." The voice trailed off. "Luckily, she has failed at it, but she has lost blood, Ma'am. We are arranging for the blood type. But you need to come as soon as possible."

Smriti let out a shriek.

"Hey, how could you let something like this happen under your watch? I am coming!" Smriti yelled.

She turned on the lights of her room and with quivering hands packed a suitcase of necessities. Her mind rattled with dreadful visions. Her spirit was flooded with fear.

She checked the next flight.

7:30 a.m.

Why would a strong girl like Jia do this?

Through the darting questions, she brought the blame upon herself. *Maybe my not calling on Sunday made her do this.*

Her heart lurched to the lowest of dungeons.

She turned on the shower over her head. The water cascaded through her face, taking her streaming tears down with it. She sat on the bathroom floor, hugging her knees, and wailed.

Visions of Jia falling from the terrace, or hanging from somewhere …

"Please God, please, let my daughter live. I will never think of myself again. I will devote every minute of every day to Jia. Please take care of her. I beg you. Please."

She rushed to the airport after purchasing a ticket.

Jia's smiling face flashed before her eyes. How had her maternal intuition skipped her?

How could I be fooled by a teenager's excitement to explore the world? Of course I shouldn't have sent her away from me! Have I learnt nothing from my own experience? Smriti's mind rattled with thoughts.

She landed in Indore and rushed to the hospital.

Jia was in the ICU. As she saw her, she lost balance. Her heartthrob, the muffin she had given birth to, the princess she had read fairy tales to, her best friend, the story of her life, was lying on the bed with bandages on her wrist. An IV needle was inserted in her veins.

With each step heavier than the other, she headed towards the bed.

"Please God, please …" she murmured again.

The scene was blinding. The blade with which she had slit her wrists was lying in a plastic zip-lock on the table. A note was right next to it.

"Please tell Mummy I am sorry. I could not cope up."

Smriti let out a loud howl.

"She lost blood. It took a few hours to arrange her blood type, AB negative. She was rushed in at night. We hope that her body accepts the blood without any reaction," the doctor explained as he heard Smriti's cry.

"Save her, doctor," she cried, wretched to the stomach.

"She should regain consciousness soon. You should counsel her and keep her close to you after this," the doctor replied sternly.

Smriti walked out of the ICU. She saw that her school principal and teacher were sitting on a bench. A girl was sitting with them.

"This girl had gone to the bathroom in the middle of the night and found Jia unconscious. She was lying on the wet floor with blood leaking through her wrists. She has saved her."

"My daughter is battling for her life and all you have is a story for me?" she yelled at the principal.

Smriti went inside the bathroom and vomited, howling till her stomach hurt. Jia had tried to take her life – even a million yells could not create the space to let that sink in.

She went back to talk to that girl.

"Srishti, right?" Smriti whispered, looking at her.

"Yes Ma'am," Srishti replied, surprised that Jia's mother knew about her.

"Can I have a word please?" Smriti needed to get to the bottom of why her daughter had taken such an extreme step. There was strength in her spirit to fight this, to pray life into her daughter.

"Yes Ma'am." Srishti walked her to the side.

"What was bothering her?"

"The bullies. They have been bullying her ever since she joined school," Srishti said.

"They have been bullying her? She said they were bullying you!" Smriti voice was filled with anguish. "Was she trying to stand up for you? Was that why they singled her out?" Smriti was apologetic for her outright interrogation, but a mother's worst fear was triggered. "Was it because she doesn't have a father? Is that why she was targeted?"

"Oh. She told us that her father is in the navy …" Srishti gulped down the reason why Jia was made the target. "And no, Ma'am. They never bullied me. Jia was uneasy telling you about the bullying, so she must have taken my name. They have been bullying her a lot. You know, they stole things and said Jia had done it. Though everyone knows it is them, nobody stands up against it. People play along, mocking and keeping distance from their targets. They pressed her breasts with their shoes till she started crying. She complained to the teachers and it got even worse. They have asked the batch to ignore her. They laugh at her all the time." Srishti's voice faded. She turned her head toward the floor.

"Tell, me more. What is it that led her to take such a step?" Smriti was shaking with fear and anger. Her eyes were sore from the crying; her throat was hurting from the excessive vomiting.

"When she got her period, they put ketchup on her sheets. She washed her sheets through her period despite the chum pain. They put red paint on pads and pasted them inside her closet. That broke her. It haunted her." Srishti's chest caved inward.

"What were you, as her friend, doing all this while?!" All the while she was telling Jia not to stand up for her friend if that brought trouble to her, and it was Jia going through everything alone!

How could her heart not know?

Insufficiency ate her up. Visions of Jia lying on that bed, unconscious, fighting her desire of death, afraid to wake up into this world that had shown her suffering, were filling her brain with the breadcrumbs. She must have lost faith along with her blood. Jia was lonely, even though there was a mother who lived for her.

There was strength in her spirit to fight this, to pray life into her daughter.

Guilt, distress, and trepidation, were met by a light in Smriti's energy. A light and strength that was lit by her time with Keshav. After a moment of reflection and absorption, Smriti felt empowered. She had to pull her baby out of bed.

Smriti's eyes brimmed with tears.

"I am sorry, Ma'am. If we talk to anyone who is being bullied, we get bullied too. In fact, I tried talking to her and taking her side, but I was called a –" Srishti paused before continuing, "a lesbian for doing so. Anya and I were teased for being Jia's *lovers* and then we had to stop talking to her. Sorry, Ma'am …"

These teenagers are revolting, Smriti thought as she walked into the ICU again.

She approached the Jia's bed and sat beside it. She placed her palm on Jia's forehead.

Jia is okay, she told herself. *Jia is okay*, she repeated. With her eyes closed, she imagined rays of white light entering and strengthening Jia's body. She affirmed, till the universe believed it.

It took another hour, but the doctor's voice broke her prayers.

"Jia will be stable soon." he told her.

Smriti waited outside the ICU and drank water. The distress had dried her up and bile had cast a sourness in her system.

I will never let her out of my sight again, she thought. *How had this sensitive soul harbored the toxicity of guile teenagers?*

Smriti waited, pacing up and down the hospital wing with quivering knees. Her phone buzzed with Keshav's messages. She did not reply to them. The sun had set, it had been a long day, and Jia was yet to regain consciousness.

Her mind drifted to the day she decided to keep her pregnancy, overcoming a million struggles. The voices of her parents asking her not to be foolish, her father threatening to break contact with her if she kept the child, the first sonography, and the beating heart that had made the doubts and voices of her family vanish. Soon, Smriti's life revolved around baby Jia, who'd need a fresh story every mealtime to eat, who was styled as Radha in her school's annual day performance when she was five.

Smriti buried her face in her hands and sat outside the ICU.

Finally, at 8:00 p.m., the doctor announced, "Jia is awake now."

Smriti rushed into the room.

"Jia!" she whispered.

Jia's curly hair was muddled, and her lips were parched. The little teenage acne that had popped on her cheeks was drained color.

Her hazel eyes lit up. The longing to see the one person she loved, was furnished. She smiled but couldn't meet her mother's eyes. She looked down and ironed the creases of her hospital gown.

"Are you okay, Jia?" Smriti asked, cradling Jia into her arms.

Jia didn't reply; she was groggy.

Smriti cried, "Please talk to me. I beg of you."

Jia traced Smriti's neckline as her head hit Smriti's bosom. The fabric was gentle against her cheek – her mother never changed her garment vendor.

"Mummy, you forgot to call me on Sunday!" Jia whispered in her meek voice.

"I am so sorry my bacha. I am so sorry. I did not forget; I was in a no-network zone. I am so sorry!"

"Where did you go?"

"I had gone for a trek … Lohargarh Fort," Smriti replied, filled with guilt.

"*Array wah.* (Oh wow!) With that group of yours?"

"Yes. You wanted to leave your Mumma alone? Why beta?" Smriti asked her tenderly, playing with her curls.

"I don't want to go back there, Mumma," Jia said in a hushed tone. She had little energy to cry.

"*Ghar jayenge bas yahaan se* (We'll go straight home from here). Are you alright?"

"Feeling weak and dizzy," Jia murmured.

"You've lost blood. It will take a while for your wrist to heal and for you to regain your strength," Smriti spoke in a stable tone, moving toward the bed's edge. She rubbed Jia's feet and fiddled with her toes affectionately.

Smriti hummed a song.

"You sang this song during our last dinner together," Jia recalled.

"Yes, before you resumed school after summer." Smriti smiled, recalling their evening.

"What boring music you listen to, Mummy!" Jia had said when Smriti hummed the song.

"The lyrics are beautiful, listen to them! *Tum haar k dil apna, meri jeet amar kardo ...*"

"Haan the lyrics are nice. But they are such slow songs! You're a romantic, Mummy!" Jia had teased.

"I fell in love and had a child without marriage – of course I'm a romantic!" Smriti had blushed.

Jia nodded.

Jia had thought about Smriti before flicking the blade from the pottery room. But she lost trail of it when she was ambushed with the excessive bullying. When she had opened her cupboards, there were pads sprayed with red paint, and the blade was on the top shelf. She'd found an escape from the mess.

But sitting in the hospital, she wondered, *how did I forget my mother's sacrifices?*

Jia's mouth and throat were dry from the medication. Guilt made it coarse. She gulped the little saliva that lined her mouth to balm her throat.

Winding up the day, Smriti spoke with the doctor.

"I'm not sure of the extent of bullying that has taken place, but a child trying to take their life should not be left unattended or unheard. Apart from your constant care and support, you must send Jia for counselling," the doctor explained to Smriti.

"I will, Doctor. Do we need to give her any medication?" Smriti asked.

"A psychiatrist would be a better judge of that. Kindly send her to a counsellor and let them judge the extent to which she needs assistance." Standing outside the ICU, having more patients than he could handle, the doctor was exhausted. The principal was also sitting outside the ICU, waiting for Jia to wake up.

"Children need therapy as much as adults do. They are at such a supple age; they must be protected from such experiences. In fact, not just the one who gets bullied – the bullies need therapy too. We need to understand narcissistic behavior right from the beginning, otherwise it will manifest with age. Principal Ma'am, please take this up earnestly. You must have an in-school therapist or counsellor, someone who can connect with these children and guide them. You're keeping them away from their families; it is your duty to provide them with the care they need."

As the doctor walked away, Smriti spoke with the principal.

"How could the matrons and house mistresses not know about it? In fact, Srishti mentioned that Jia reached out to a teacher and the bullying worsened for her. So, either your staff members are weak or simply hard-hearted! How horrible!"

"I will probe deeper into this and the culprits will be expelled. We will not take it lightly, Ma'am," the principal said, dodging eye contact.

"Though that will never undo the damage they've done to Jia, at least it could protect others from it." Smriti sighed.

Jia was moved to the hospital room. Smriti slept there with her.

Before sleeping, she thought about how she had done everything in her power to give her a good upbringing and education to secure her future; she had done everything in her life for Jia, spent every minute of every day to provide and care for her. And the one time in life when she had done something for herself – lightning had struck them down. A single slip-up. A single slip-up was all it had taken to splatter their lives away.

There were pending messages and missed calls from Keshav.

"I am worried now," Keshav's evening message read.

She wanted to tell him what had happened, to continue sharing her life with him, because honestly, she had fallen in love. But she knew that would distract her. She could not afford that. Jia needed her unwavering attention. She ignored his messages and calls. She knew what she had to do with their relationship. But she did not have the strength that day.

It's true, Keshav did not deserve this. Their relationship did not deserve this. But that day, she was grateful that her daughter was alive. She remembered her morning prayer. She was never going to choose herself above her maternal duties.

They stayed in the hospital for another two days. Smriti read Jia a novel to keep her occupied.

"The tea they're serving here will make even a healthy person sick," Smriti said, dumping her cup in the dustbin.

"*Aap lessons lelo* (You take lessons) … "Jia replied.

"Haan bas yahan se nikalke, yehi plan hai … poore duniya ko chai banana sikhaungi (Yes, once we leave from here … I'll teach the world how to make good tea)!" Smriti said, giggling.

I am witty because of you Keshav, thank you … Smriti thought. She acknowledged a stronger spirit because of the joy Keshav had left her with. The skipped heartbeats were becoming the boat to sail upon through life's turbulence.

Jia looked at the lunch served to her. She twirled the *daal* with her spoon. "Food also, please." She pushed the plate away. "I don't feel like eating anything …"

"*Thoda sa khaa lo* (Eat a little bit). You need energy, beta." Smriti brushed Jia's head with her fingers. She kissed her head. "You have gone through a lot."

"I am scared of people now, Mummy," Jia confessed. The laughter of the mean girls from when they saw her crying and washing her sheets still rang in her ears. She cloaked the real reason why she was the target of the school. She was not ready to share it with anyone.

"We will work everything out together. You will trust people again, I promise. The right people will come by to gain your trust. And we will walk together into the light."

Smriti fed Jia her meals. Her phone rang with Keshav's call.

"*I am worried Smriti, please reply,*" his message buzzed on her phone.

"*Please give me two days. I am with her in Indore. I will get back to you,*" she replied firmly.

They left the hospital, Smriti holding Jia's hand. The slit on Jia's left wrist was bandaged. Jia waited outside while Smriti went into the boarding school.

She packed Jia's belongings in her trunk. Luckily, Jia's dormmates were in class, and the dorm was empty. After clearing her cupboard out, she went to her bed. The closet had remnant marks of cello-tape being pulled out. *It's where the painted pads would have been stuck.*

She collected the items that lay on her bedside. Her pillow was stained with tear marks. And under the pillow she found a picture of the two of them.

Jia had written about a friend of hers keeping pictures under her pillow, Smriti recalled.

They took a flight back to Mumbai. Jia placed her head on Smriti's shoulders and napped through the flight.

Reaching the apartment, Jia pushed the door open. Home smelled of her mother's cooking. Her eyes landed on the heart-warming pictures in the living room.

Wow, Jia thought, looking around the familiar space. "Your plants have grown! And you still have that clock hanging!"

"It's still working! Why throw it out?" Smriti replied. Her eyes went to the mini Merlion that Keshav had made for her during pottery class. Maintaining a poker face, she ushered the luggage inside.

"I missed you, Booh." Jia picked up a soft bear she had had since she was four.

Smriti went into the kitchen to prepare *khichdi* for dinner. She tempered it with a heavy desi ghee *tadka* to heal Jia's wounds.

Mummy is shelter, Jia thought as she relished her homely dinner. Smriti gave her a glass of turmeric milk after dinner. She slept within minutes of hitting her bed. The nightmares spared Jia that night – her childhood home, her soft toys, and her mother had her back.

Seeing that Jia was snug, content about having her back, Smriti turned to face the looming missed calls and messages.

I cannot tell him what happened, it's not my story, Smriti contemplated. *Shall I tell him I love him? No … he will stay hung up …*

She sat on the bench and dialed his number.

"Where have you been, Smriti? Please tell me everything is alright."

"Hey Keshav. Everything is alright now. She was being bullied at school …"

"Oh, I'm sorry! I hope you've gotten her back then?"

"I have."

"What happened, Smriti?"

"She is my life, Keshav. And the truth is, our relationship, yours and mine, is distracting me from my duties."

"But that's not how it should be, right? You should balance both, Smriti."

"I was unable to. It has been two months and I have already failed at it."

"Jia being bullied was not your fault."

There was a pause. Smriti paced around the terrace.

"You've called up to end this ..."

"Yes. You know I don't want to."

"Yes, I do understand. Does it make sense to say that I will wait for you, *Remembrance?*"

"Please don't, Keshav … You made me see a new version of myself, and I am forever grateful. Things were gloomy before you came. But now, I'm filled with strength. I laugh now …"

"I would be incomplete without you now. I want to be with you, Smriti. Please take time to settle her and come back?"

"I want to say I will, Keshav. But I won't. I can't make a commitment I'm not confident about. There is a bleak chance that we will meet again. Maybe in another life."

"My heart is aching."

"I'm sorry."

She cut the call and cried. She had let go off the person who had brought her back to life. She pulled her knees close to her, and held onto the joy and love they shared.

"Micchāmi Dukkadam," she sent out to him – forgive my mistakes.

CHAPTER SIX

The ticking of the clock
Synchronizes with the heartbeat
Why is it such a wonder then
That time heals wounds

TO KESHAV, THE reason of their break-up remained ambiguous. He resumed what he knew best – work. He buried himself with projects, so he got little time to contemplate his heartbreak.

"Yes, the investor-start-up fit is perfect," he told his colleague. "The founder is middle-aged and has knowledge about his product. What he needs apart from funding is a leverage in technology and business development. He can increase his addressable market size with a good website and marketing. Let's see it through! How much equity is he willing to let go?"

"20%. It is too less for his ask. He needs to dilute at least one-third of the company. Only then will those investors want in. They've made it clear," his colleague said.

"Okay, I'll speak with the founder," Keshav said.

"There are companies that need your attention, Keshav. Silktro was about to come out with a public offer, but it got stuck with paperwork."

"Have they informed us? We hold stakes in them!" Keshav said, surprised the matter wasn't in his notice.

"Yes, you hold a 10% stake in it, and I hold a 5% stake. Here are the documents, they sent them while you were in Mumbai."

"Why public offer? Why do they need more money?"

"They want to set up units … manufacturing in Bangladesh."

"Why do they need company-owned units, they can outsource. The entire lifestyle industry is working through job workers, and these guys want their own factories … There is a difference between being aggressive and being reckless. These founders don't care about the funds because it is not theirs." Keshav was irritated. He got up from his seat and paced the office.

"What should we do about it?" his colleague asked. "Should we call them in for a meeting?"

"Definitely. I need to know in detail why they want public funds. But we need to do something substantial about these things. We need to build an 'ARA: Accountability, Responsibility, and Answerability' understanding in founders."

He sat down again, twisted his pen between his fingers, and swirled in his chair. He surfed through his pending emails. Amidst the many emails, there was one from Singapore University. He clicked on it.

"We invite you to mentor our students, in our bi-annual Student-preneur Programs."

His eyes lit up as he went through the specifics of the mail: an invitation to mentor college students.

He sent his acceptance of the position.

***

Smriti and Jia solved their life one step at a time.

In the state she had brought Jia back, Smriti could not leave her at home alone while she went to work. She chalked out a schedule with her seniors. Her innately consistent and sincere nature worked to her benefit.

Jia had to be readmitted into another school.

They went from one school to another, requesting them to take her in. But they found no respite. There were no schools which were taking Jia mid-session and that too in a senior class. They waited for hours outside various principals' offices, trying to explain what they had gone through and why they should admit her in their school.

But they were politely refused a seat everywhere they went. With the initial ones, Smriti explained Jia's reasons for leaving the previous school, and it worked against them. Smriti sensed they did not want a student of weak mental health to join them. Disheartened, they adapted to the technique of artificial talks and smiles – the cover-up-your-weakness-in-public kind of approach. Yet, they faced rejection.

Another tough task was to acquaint Jia with a counsellor.

"Mummy, I don't need therapy," Jia replied when Smriti told her about the scheduled session.

"Beta, you do need help. Talk about things that bother you. There is no guarantee that life won't be harsh again or that people would be kinder. I've gone through rough patches. Taking your life is not the solution to people's rash behavior. You have to get stronger, resilient, and you need the right kind of assistance for it," Smriti explained.

"You trusted that a boarding school would be a better environment than home, and now you trust that a counsellor would do a better job than you," Jia whispered.

Smriti swallowed the lump in her throat.

"I am sorry. I am sorry that I sent you there," Smriti said. "I promise I will be around. But that is not enough. You should have someone with whom you can speak about topics you are uncomfortable sharing with me. And you need to get stronger. Please, give the counsellor a chance," Smriti insisted, putting up a strong protest.

"I'm telling you it is useless," Jia said, "but I will give it a shot if that makes you feel better."

She went for her session.

"Do you want to talk about your first memory of the bullying?" the therapist asked her.

"No," Jia replied.

"Would you like to tell me the names of the bullies?"

"I don't want to speak about anything." Jia glanced around her office, noticing the certificates hanging on the wall.

She's here because she's getting paid, Jia thought, *not because she cares about me.*

"Do you want to talk about your childhood?" the therapist asked. "You can share a pleasant memory from your childhood."

Jia did not reply. She stayed quiet for the session.

When she came out of the session and sat in the car with Smriti, she muttered, "There, you spilled your money on strangers, again." She rolled her eyes and put on loud music.

Once they were home, she went straight to her bedroom.

Smriti rushed behind her. "You have to speak to someone …"

"I don't want someone to listen to me because they're being paid for it," Jia said angrily and shut her room's door.

She put on her hard rock music and sketched recklessly in her drawing book.

When she came out of her room for dinner, Smriti broke down.

"Don't cry. I went to the therapist because you told me to. But really, I do not need 'talking' or 'counselling', I need someone to be there. I need you to be there. Nobody else. Everything will be okay if you are around."

What do I even tell the therapist? Jia contemplated. *Nobody can understand me, I can't understand myself. My life has always been incomplete … and now, I'm even more complex.*

"Please promise me that things will get alright." Smriti cried, tired of battling life, wishing with every breath she heaved that things would get easier. "Please promise me that you will never think of such extreme ideas again."

"No, never again, Mom," Jia promised. "I will go to the therapist again, but I'm telling you, she can't do anything for me."

Nobody can do anything for me. I have to figure myself out. And you have to love me and be there for me, Jia thought.

During her next counselling session, Jia spoke to the therapist in a series of monosyllables.

"What do you want to speak about?" Jia asked impatiently, as she sat with the therapist.

"Whatever bothers you, Jia," the therapist said.

"Too many things bother me … and at times, nothing bothers me," Jia replied.

"Let's begin with one thing at a time," the therapist said.

"There's nothing I want to speak with you about," Jia stated bluntly.

"Let's speak about the weather then," the therapist tried.

Yeah, kill your forty-five minutes on weather and get paid for it, Jia thought, irritated.

"Mumbai's weather is good. I enjoy the humidity, grew up with it. Would you like to speak about any other city?" Jia replied, rolling her eyes.

The same continued for the remaining session.

The therapist had a private word with Smriti after their session.

"There is a lot in there that needs to be healed, it is not just the bullying … I don't know what it is, but we'll get there slowly. Take care of her …"

Smriti nodded, taking Jia's hand in hers.

"Thank you for at least trying this," Smriti said.

On their way back, they stopped at a bookstore. The scent of bound printed paper pierced through their humdrum.

"It is Diwali tomorrow; do you remember our deal?" Smriti asked Jia.

"Yes …" Jia said.

They walked to the mythology section and picked up a book on Indian Goddesses.

They spent the evening making pizzas together and reading about the divine feminine energy.

"I am the sovereign queen, the treasury of all treasures,
Whose breathing forth gives birth to all the worlds and yet
Extends beyond them – so vast am I in greatness"
Devi Sukta (Praise Hymn of the Goddess): Rig Veda

***

"Don't nudge him into Commerce. He should study Science in school; after that he can change his field," Neha told Keshav.

"He should study whatever he wants to, Neha! His career will be built if he enjoys his work," Keshav protested.

"You're saying this because you work in the start-up space, Keshav," Neha replied.

"We both can put our perspectives, but eventually his field should be his decision. Is there any chance of him studying in Singapore? I'm going to mentor at the Singapore University. He'll get international exposure and stay at home with me," Keshav asked.

"No, India is fine. It has good engineering colleges. Besides, I can't do the distance," Neha replied curtly.

Well, I'm doing it, Keshav thought to himself.

"I've booked his return flight for the 18th," Keshav informed her, turning toward Kaveer and making a sad face.

Kaveer shrugged. "Hang up now!"

Kaveer's trip to Singapore was ending. In the previous week, Keshav had taken Kaveer for a concert, put-put golf, a science exhibition, experiential fine dining, everything that he could fit into the one week Kaveer was with him.

It was Diwali and they were exploring Singapore's Little India celebrations. They strolled through the lit-up bazaar, stopping to watch folk dance street shows and singers in the foreign land.

"Their expressions are vivid," Kaveer said, gelato dripping from his hand as he watched them with awe.

"You must have seen Kathakali events in Kerala," Keshav said.

"Yes, I have a friend who does Kathak professionally," Kaveer told Keshav. "He comes from one of those artist families. He invites us for his performances. The days he dances, he skips school because it takes time to put on the costume and apply make-up."

"Does he enjoy dancing? Or does he do it for his family?" Keshav asked.

"He loves it."

"That would make him a brilliant dancer!" Keshav said. He ran his hand through Kaveer's hair, gel sticking to his fingers.

"What is this that you apply? Will it improve my hair loss?" Keshav asked.

"Not at all, it is going to make you lose all of it." Kaveer laughed. "You're getting funnier by the year. And *mota*, Papa." He poked a finger into his belly.

"Yeah, I have to start exercising. Anyway, tell me more about your life, I miss out on so much of it," Keshav said. "Which football team do you support?"

"Man-U all the way," Kaveer said. "We gather in the colony and watch them together. Did you see the last match? That last goal was so cool! But also, Mummy complains on all match days. She keeps calling me up till I'm back home. Everyone makes fun of me."

"It's okay. She worries about you. Next summer, do you want to go to London to see one of the matches live?" Keshav asked.

"Wow! That would be sick," Kaveer said.

"Sick?" Keshav asked, bewildered. "I thought it was a good thing, why would it be sick?"

Kaveer laughed. "Sick means awesome!"

Keshav and Kaveer spent the next day playing on the PlayStation.

"Tell me things about Singapore, Papa," Kaveer asked while playing on the PlayStation.

"Singapore was a third world country and has developed into a first world country recently. Lee Kuan Yew, the first Prime Minister after independence from the British and a split from Malaysia, worked hard to establish Singapore on the world map," Keshav told Kaveer. "Today, Singapore's per capita GDP is higher than the USA's."

"I think the small size and population must have worked to its benefit," Kaveer said, adding, "India's population is huge. It takes longer to implement policies."

"Correct," Keshav replied. "Do you enjoy reading the news?"

"Some geo-political news … I wish my school had better exposure in Humanities – even the teachers teach as if the subjects are unimportant!"

"I will look for some online classes for you. Now go on, pack your suitcase, you're leaving in a day."

"The vacation has been insane, Papa. I don't want to go back," Kaveer said. "I will come back during the winter vacation. Spend Christmas here, and New Year's Eve with Mummy."

"I feel all alone without you," Keshav admitted. Tears brimmed in his eyes. Kaveer gave him a hug and said, "You're a superhero, Papa, and superheroes don't cry …"

When Kaveer went back, Keshav framed pictures of his old family and placed them in his living room.

***

"Hello Samir, I am unable to continue with the support group meetings. Please give my love to everyone," Smriti texted in response to Samir's missed call.

"Hi Lata, I cannot meet up for a while, brought Jia back from the boarding school," Smriti texted Lata in response to her calls.

One workday after another, one school visit after another, one counselling session after another, months slipped away for Smriti and Jia.

I wish I could spend the day with Jia, time away is going to make things worse for her, Smriti thought, typing on her laptop in office, *but I am both, the mother and the father.*

She made 1:00 p.m. touch-base calls to Jia from work.

"I'm okay, Mummy," Jia said everyday, even though her head throbbed with memories of the bullying. She remembered how it had started – a side of her she wished never existed, the side of her she wished to destroy with the blade she had flicked from the pottery class. The many nights she sketched sitting in the bathroom.

Amidst everything, Smriti was left with less energy to think about how her life had changed in two months' time. She had no time or energy during the day to reminisce about her time with Keshav. It was only after Jia went to bed that Smriti sat in her sofa and thought about her time with Keshav and how easy she felt with him.

She wondered how he was. They were always going to stay connected through the moments they had shared together. Those moments had their place in the cosmic world. Yet, they were distant.

After months of school hunting, juggling work, managing the wrecked nerves of two people, scheduled therapy sessions, Smriti was exhausted. She put up a strong face, nurturing Jia's spirits, while she was crumbling from within.

One day, after Jia slept, Smriti went up to the terrace. She watched the January clouds shield the stars and smiled remembering Keshav's interesting observation of the moon. The businessman had been artistic.

"What to do, Keshav, we're unable to find a school for her," Smriti thought, exasperated. She buried her face in her palms.

In Singapore, Keshav was being covered by the media every day, but he had no one to share his success with. He had gone out for dinner with some colleagues to celebrate the profit they had made by selling a start-up. They ordered sushi that night. He diluted the wasabi in his soy and spread it over his sushi.

"Always with you, Smriti," he whispered in a hushed voice, wondering how she was doing.

In an instant, sitting in Mumbai, Smriti felt relieved. Her soul shimmered with cosmic comfort. As if after a terrible day, Keshav had made her laugh.

She woke up the next day and tried the last school they had on her their list.

If this doesn't work out, I'll have to quit work and home-school her, Smriti thought.

"You seem to be in luck, Ma'am. One of our student's parents have decided to move abroad and have withdrawn their son. We do have a spot open," the principal announced in a seraphic voice.

"When can she join, Ma'am?" Smriti asked, with gleaming eyes.

"Come tomorrow itself. You've missed enough of school."

Smriti and Jia looked at each other excitedly.

The moment they left the school, they hugged tightly.

"Unbelievable," Jia said. "This was the last school on our list, right?"

Smriti nodded.

To celebrate the evening before Jia joined school, Smriti took her to Colaba.

A forty-year-old single mom that would give her life for her daughter, and a fifteen-year-old girl who found comfort nowhere but by her mom's side, walked through the dusk-lit streets of Mumbai.

"Let's do something fun together, Mumma!" Jia exclaimed.

"Yes, we have something due." Smriti reminisced about Keshav's kiss on her earlobes.

Smriti glanced at the place "Tattoos and Piercings". She held Jia's hand and led her into the small, dimly-lit place.

"Are you sure you want to do this?" Jia asked Smriti, gulping her rising excitement.

Smriti nodded.

"Do you want to get one done?" Smriti asked Jia.

Jia nodded. "I want to get my nose pierced."

The needle pierced through Smriti's earlobes. She bit her lip to curb the yell.

"Is it meant to be THIS painful?" Smriti asked, her eyes wet.

"Yeah mom!" Jia replied. She let out an "ouch, ouch" as they pierced her nose.

Smriti looked at the studs they put on for her, in the mirror. She touched her earlobes.

"Wow mom, it really suits you!"

"Your nose piercing suits you too, Jia."

They walked through the streets, shopping artefacts and junk jewelry.

Sitting by the sea, sipping coffee, Jia spoke about school.

"They were the height of being nasty. Remember 'happy duniya'?"

"Yes of course I do." Smriti sighed, remembering how she had taught Jia to make a tent with her blanket. In that small world, there was nothing that could trouble her; in that small world, there was only love and joy. That "happy duniya" could be her go-to place when she missed the comfort of home.

"They saw me make my 'happy duniya' in my bed. They laughed for days about it. It has scarred me forever …" Jia vented.

"Why didn't you tell me you were being bullied?" Smriti asked.

"I didn't want to burden you …" Jia said.

"It is my duty to take care of you, not the other way around," Smriti stated. She pulled Jia into her. "Jia beta … it may seem like being a single mother is difficult, and yes it probably is, but remember one thing, it has never been burdensome. Rather, it has been a beautiful journey. I love caring for you, Jia … and I want to be there for you … always."

Jia muffled her cries.

"Cry it out, beta. Happiness needs space to grow again." Smriti rubbed her shoulders as she cried.

I need to create a new "happy duniya" for her, Smriti thought.

"We'll take a holiday once you have caught up with your studies," Smriti suggested.

"Ohhhh wow! Yes, yes! Let us do that. Where would you like to go?" Jia asked.

"Want to go for a safari? Jim Corbett and Nainital?" Smriti asked with excitement.

"Oh yes, please!" Jia said, hugging Smriti. "Tigers are love!" She made a heart with her hands.

In the following days, Smriti managed both work and Jia better. She helped Jia with her homework after school. Gradually, Jia caught up on her syllabus and was faced with her year-end examinations.

***

Keshav had spoken at plenty of conferences, panel discussions, but he hadn't addressed a group of college kids before. He sat facing the first batch of student-preneurs who were shortlisted for mentorship by the university. They appeared more eager and naïve than his usual audience.

He initiated his discourse:

"To be an entrepreneur is to take the reins of one's day, and eventually one's life, into one's hands. To work for a product or purpose you relate with, for something bigger than a monthly paycheck. But how do we do that? How do we become entrepreneurs? What are the qualities of an entrepreneur? How does one gear their vision through the world? How can the resilience and dynamism needed in a founder be developed? How can we maintain these qualities when faced with the ups and downs of a business? How should an entrepreneur develop his uniqueness? This is what you and I will work towards in the coming months."

They presented their ideas one by one.

Keshav was assigned a student-preneur. He watched the naïve kids preparing to step out into the world.

Kaveer and Lily would be one of them, somewhere … Smriti's kid too, Keshav thought as he took on his start-up.

***

Jia fared adequately in her exams and was promoted to the next grade, Class Eleven. During the session break, Jia and Smriti took their promised holiday together.

It was spring, both in season and in their lives.

They spent two nights in Nainital before heading to Jim Corbett. They walked around the Tibetan markets and the Mall Road, shopping trinkets and feng shui coins. They ate their meals at quaint cafés.

Smriti put her arm around Jia, who was an inch taller than her now.

"I'm going to have to protect you from boys now, you're growing up beautiful."

Jia cringed, her lips curling up in a strained smile, and she did not say anything.

They went boating at the Naini Lake. Nestled between the mountains, the lake was a bank of sights. With tourists buzzing and bargaining with rowboat assistants, the chirping of the birds and the hum of the lake could be heard by those who wanted to listen to nature. The snow-covered peaks stood strongly above them, embracing them into a wholesome reality.

Jia was washed by an unmatched serenity. After everything she had gone through, she needed that oxygen flowing through her. She needed the chirp of the birds, the rustle of the wind, and the splashes of the lake.

Jia photographed the mountains, the boatmen, and the soaring birds. Smriti bent down to touch the lake while the boat was sailing. The cold water brushed her fingertips. Smriti hummed a song. Jia recorded a video of Smriti.

Nainital was followed by Jim Corbett. They stayed in a small cottage and went for safaris both in the morning and in the evening. Following pugmarks and the hustle of the deer, they scouted for tiger sightings. The excitement and the thrill of finding a tiger hidden behind the bushes filled them with freshness.

"Bhaiya, ek bhi tiger nahi dikha (we haven't seen a single tiger) ..." Jia complained to the guide.

"Kya kare Madam, Mausam aisa hai … ped bhi ghane hai, aur tiger ko pyaas bhi nahi lagti … garmi mein dikhte hai araam se, paani peene bahaar aate hai na, (What can be done Madam, the weather is such …trees are in full bloom and the tigers don't feel thirsty … it's easy to spot them in summer when they come out to drink water)," the tour guide replied.

As they were about to exit the reserve on their last safari, they saw jeeps huddled at a spot.

"Hush, he is hunting," someone whispered.

Jia peered into the woods. Smriti lifted her sunglasses to get a better look.

Jia tugged at Smriti's sleeve. They saw him.

Smriti whispered, "I forgot how beautiful they are."

"Me too," Jia said, rearranging the cap she was wearing over her curls.

The formidable facial expression, the burning eyes … He sprinted with powerful movements and leaped. They heard the sway of trees, the deer's hustle, and then a short bawl. Birds twittered and hovered over the site.

Smriti and Jia exchanged looks.

Faced with nature's candor, the circles of life, they wound up their trip.

Back at school, Jia rediscovered her passion for fine arts and designing.

Jia recreated the tiger's expression in her art and sketched Smriti's portrait from her memories of Nainital.

She had started speaking to her therapist, and that helped her deal with the haunting memories.

Smriti's routine revolved around her duties, allowing little scope for wanderlust and even self-care. Abiding by her resolution, Smriti had not spoken to Keshav in six months, but she thought about him every day.

Amidst their days, Smriti wrote stories for children. Jia sketched along with the stories. Smriti wrote them with the intent to morally educate and positively influence children. Jia sketched as her mother wrote, pairing the stories with cartoons and drawings.

"Roro, the cow, ate leaves for breakfast, lunch, and dinner. One day, a leaf got stuck in his nose. 'Aachhoo aachhoo,' he sneezed, but the leaf did not come out. It itched. Then Kiki, the monkey, came along, he took Roro to the doctor …" her stories read, and Jia drew animated sketches to match her mum's stories.

They penned and sketched into the night.

"Mum, did you hear from my father?" Jia asked Smriti.

"No," Smriti replied. "Do you think a lot about it? Does it bother you?"

"No, not much," Jia replied. "It stopped bothering me in school itself."

"Why did you tell the kids in your school that your father is in the navy?" Smriti confronted Jia.

"I've been saying that for many years now. It is easier than telling them the truth," Jia divulged. "But tell me, Mumma, it must not have been easy staying single all this while."

Smriti looked at her, blinked rapidly, and turned back to her writing.

"Did you meet anyone after Tushar?" Jia asked Smriti in a melodious tone.

Smriti got up and went to cook dinner for both of them.

"Say *na*, Mumma …" Jia insisted.

"I met someone in a dream once," Smriti muttered.

"If you find someone, I wouldn't mind." Jia smiled as she said the words, looking down at her sketch and continuing to work to avoid any mutual awkwardness.

"Hush, you're getting older by the day, aren't you!" Smriti said, maintaining the tone, even though her heart was pounding hard. "How was the meeting with the counsellor?" Smriti changed the topic.

"It was fine." Jia accepted the change of topic. "We'll become friends."

After Jia slept, Smriti went to the terrace.

Tears streamed down her face. *She sees my sacrifice … she sees my life …* Smriti thought. *My daughter has grown up … I can tell her about Keshav.*

She paced the terrace in excitement. She thought about their support group meetings. She wondered if Mahesh had gotten someone to wrestle with, and if Samir was still leading the group, and the rest – Tuhina, Juhi, Seema.

After almost a year of restraint, she could now speak with Keshav.

Ecstatic, she high-fived herself like a young girl.

I will look for the right time and tell Jia, Smriti decided within herself. *Would he have moved on, found someone else?*

After office, Smriti and Jia wrote another story together. By now they had written forty children's stories together. Their stories were written to influence children to be empathetic, kind-hearted, believers, and creative.

"Let's have dinner with Lata Aunty and her family next Sunday? She has been asking me to meet them since forever, but I wasn't sure you were ready to chit chat with others. Are you ready now?" Smriti asked Jia.

"Mm-hmm. We can give it a shot. Sunday sounds okay," Jia replied.

"How do you think we can publish this?" Jia asked Smriti, glancing at the substantial pile their hobby had created.

"I have no clue, dear. We'll figure it out with time …" Smriti replied.

"Alright, let it be home décor till then!" Jia grinned.

Smriti smiled; the toughest was behind her. There it was – the light at the end of the tunnel – waiting for her to take the last few steps toward it. She glanced outside the window. It was drizzling. Mumbai appeared resplendent through the prisms of those monsoon water droplets.

I will call him tomorrow, she thought and cross-checked his contact number. Knowing that his comforting voice was a call away now, she slept like a log.

Smriti woke up, happier.

Jia's school bus had not come because of the incessant rainfall.

"Do you need to go to school today?" Smriti asked Jia, examining the logging water.

"Yes, I have a presentation!" Jia said.

"Okay. What time do you get off school? I will come from office," Smriti asked.

"I get off at 3:30 p.m.," Jia confirmed, packing her bag and tiffin.

Smriti got into the car to drop Jia. "Baby, I am not getting a good feeling. We should go back home today." Smriti's time had taught her that Mumbai was the prettiest during its rains and the scariest during its floods.

"*Aap chalo* (Let's go). We are five minutes away," Jia insisted. "School bell is about to ring …*presentation first class mein hai* (the presentation is in the first class)."

Smriti dropped Jia off to school and went to office.

The sky was filled with gray, but Smriti was as bright as she could be. She hummed in office, looking at herself in the mirror and wondering if she had aged in the past year. Now the year was about to end. Their separation phase was about to finish.

Will he forgive me for my absence? Will he understand why I chose duty over love? Does he still feel the same way? Would he like to be together for the rest of our lives? Maybe I can propose to him this time!

Smriti's mind ran in several directions.

Smriti typed faster on her laptop, hoping that the day would pass by quickly and she'd be on call with Keshav.

3:00 p.m.

She sat in her car.

The road was flooded till the shin. On reaching midway, her car stopped. She restarted it. *God bless this oldie of a car,* she thought, driving to Jia's school. *I should replace it now.*

She saw the time. 3:15 p.m. Jia would be free in fifteen minutes.

My ancestral property in Lucknow is sizeable … I can sell that and use it for Jia's college. And then the Mumbai flat is another property that I could sell to resettle near Keshav, Smriti contemplated.

Jia was waiting outside school.

"The presentation did not happen today. *Koi nahi aaya aaj* (nobody came today), you were right," Jia told her.

"I told you so," Smriti told Jia. "To reach back is a task, the water level is rising."

Jia made Smriti meet a classmate. "Neena. What a pretty name you have. You must come by to our place," Smriti said. "Have your parents come to pick you up?"

"No, they want to wait for the water level to reduce. In front of our house, the flood height has reached four feet. Jia, please be careful while going back."

"Our house is two kilometers away. We will walk it if our car gets stuck," Jia told Neena. "How will you stay here though? Do you want to come with us?" she offered as they walked towards their car.

"I will wait inside the school for my parents to come by," Neena politely refused.

It was 4:00 p.m. The tides were tilting.

Another cloud burst and the rain turned into a tempest. The water was pouring at a hitting speed, and the floods fostered higher.

"We should rush now," Smriti said, getting jittery. *Two kilometers,* she judged.

They ran to their hatchback and drove.

Water seeped through the doors into the car. Their feet were immersed in water. Smriti accelerated through the first kilometer.

The water was at waist-level now. The roads were deserted.

In minutes, the rainwater reached up to the window panes, covering the car. The hatchback gave up. Smriti tried the ignition, again and again. But it did not have the horsepower to pull through.

"It is not budging!" she hollered. "We need to get out now!"

"We should open the doors together, or else the car will flood," Jia bellowed. "On 1, 2, 3 …"

They pushed the doors open together. Jia's door opened; rainwater gushed into the car. Smriti's door was stuck. She battled it, but it was jammed.

Water gushed in. Her nose was above the level. Smriti did not know how to breathe under water.

"Get out of the other side!" Jia screamed. She extended her arm. Smriti held onto Jia's arm and pulled herself out of the car, struggling for breath.

The skies were darker; rain was thudding against them. Smriti pulled her face and neck out. She could breathe. She was safe. One battle was won. They had to reach back safely now.

"We can't walk to the house like this, we have to get to a height!" Smriti shouted, panting.

"Yes. There, that side! Mom, I see a staircase across the street. Let's cross the road and climb those stairs." Jia pointed to the staircase.

The flood's level was shoulder-height. The clouds were shrieking; bolts of lightning were streaking the city with silvers; the clamor of the torrent was deafening.

They walked one step at a time, crossing the road. They hurried, but with caution.

"You are getting slow, Mumma. Come on, hold my hand!" Jia screamed, seeing that Smriti was steps behind her.

"You go ahead. I am coming!" Smriti yelled back, fretful. She was shaking.

Afraid that the water was going to submerge her, she took one step at a time.

Jia reached the staircase and climbed up the first few stairs.

"Mummy come fast!" she yelled, waving and guiding her to the exact spot.

Smriti smiled. A few steps.

I can go back home, be with Jia. I can call Keshav up …

Suddenly, Smriti's foot slipped into nowhere. She plunged downward and was submerged under the water.

"Mummy no!" she heard Jia's scream.

Her body was straight, her feet were no longer on the ground, and she was going down. Somewhere down.

She couldn't breathe and was jetting down at a reckless speed. She was hitting something on the sides. It was a narrow tube, filled with gushing water.

She opened her eyes, but it was dark. She was cascading with the water. Her mind was blanking out. Her breath – her body was quivering. She struggled for oxygen. She was falling deeper and deeper. It was happening fast, and yet it seemed like forever. Every second without air was strangling her, making her suffer.

She moved her hands in that tube, the sides were greasy.

Manhole, she realized.

Her consciousness was slipping away. In her fleeting alertness, she wondered who Jia's guardian would be … she was a minor … whether they'd contact her father, and if it would be of any use …

She struggled for a small buff of air, but water plunged into her insides from her mouth.

God, please take care of my daughter … she's going to be alone, Smriti thought.

Her body shook with destitution.

Jia's artwork … *How can I bless her …*

Breathing was safe … and now she was gushing through the unvoyaged.

Keshav's smile, his voice singing her favorite songs with her … each word distinct in her fading mind …

It was a fight between the fall, the dark water, and her.

She had not breathed in a long time. She opened her mouth in reflex and water gushed into her insides, filling her stomach. Then it entered through her nose.

The irony of the sunlight he had filled her skies with, before the dark night was taking her away … the whiff of life she had experienced in his presence. To experience love in its most honest form, the attraction and the romance, the commitment to the emotion, the hues of ache that followed, cohesively forming the rudimentary act of love, the essence of life.

The bouts of swoon were longer than her consciousness.

I have not told him that I love him …

A blackout. She gave up the fight.

Now calm, her body hit the bottom by itself, her soul having departed it seconds before.

CHAPTER SEVEN

A story, like life
Has no measure of highs and lows
Mere faith and submission
Sails one's boat

SMRITI HAD VANISHED under the flooding water.

Forty feet above, Jia entered the flood to look for Smriti. She squabbled with the lashing rain and hunted for Smriti. The thudding rain splashed against her curly hair; wet strands stuck to her fair face, blurring her eyesight. Her hazel eyes radiated anguish, tears merging with the rainwater.

She put her head under water to scout. Squinting through the soiled water, she saw the manhole Smriti had fallen into.

The water level was rising further.

She pulled herself out of the water and climbed up the stairs, looking around for help.

It was impossible to reach the police station on foot. She could reach them through a phone. Smriti's phone had gone with her, and her phone was at home.

Walking where her intuition led her, she entered a dingy corridor, smelling of musty furniture and cigarettes. Water dripped from the damp ceiling into a well-placed rusting iron bucket. The corridor was lit by diffused sunlight of the otherwise overcast day.

The rooms were shut, but sharp laughter and banter could be heard from one of them.

Jia walked toward the specific door. She distanced herself from the sounds of the downpour. The wind blew across her body and gummed her clothes to her perfect hour-glass body; her nipples stuck out vividly through the frontal silhouette of her school shirt.

She knocked on the door; a shabbily dressed male opened it. He noticed the look of desperation and emergency. The room was filled with a weird smell. Three men were sitting on the right side of the room and sniggering.

They were on drugs. Jia's gaze met theirs, and she shivered with fear. Her destitution arose an interest within them.

"*Aap please mujhe help karo. Meri mummy paani mein doob gayi. Aapka phone use kar sakti hu police ko phone karne k liye? (*Please help me. My mother has drowned, gone down the manhole. Can any of you help me? Or I can borrow your phone to call the police)," Jia asked them in Hindi, filled with fear and innocence.

"Police." The one who opened the door laughed. "*Tumko yahaan se police ko phone karne denge?* (You think we would let you telephone the police from here?)"

The others stared at her – head to toe. She had walked into a den of ravenous men.

"Please!!" She sat down on her knees and folded her hands. The dread of things that lay behind and ahead of her, made her body quiver, exposing her hardened nipples across her shirt.

The men's eyes oozed at her petite body, drenched in rainwater.

One of the men got up from his place and grazed her wet head. He looked at her fear-filled fair face, right into her pleading eyes, and touched her cheek.

"Haan, madad karenge. Par jab phone call karoge, toh hum tumhe chhooenge, (Sure, we will help you. But when you make that phone call, we will touch you)," he jeered in a low voice. His eyes were dark with intent. He glanced back at his friends who grinned with approval.

"Please give me your phone," Jia begged.

He handed her the phone. She took it in her shaking hands and dialed 100. It went unanswered.

He was about to graze her shirt, "*Te karu naka, tila ekate soda* (Don't do that, leave her alone)," came a hiss in Marathi.

An old lady had come to drain out the brimming iron bucket. The man backed off irritably. The lady huffed at her beedi and watched over Jia as she called the police.

She dialed 100 again.

With trembling lips, Jia yelled into the phone, "Please help me. My mother has gone down a manhole. Please help me take her out of it. I beg of you." She explained the address and location.

"Ma'am, in such cases … we doubt we will find your mother," the policeman told her.

"Only if you come here can you know, right?!" Jia yelled into the phone, consolidating the happiness that her mother had given her into one ball of strength.

"Come here now!" she screamed into the phone.

"Yes, we are coming," he shot his reply.

She threw the phone at the jeering impious men and ran outside. The old lady picked up her bucket and left.

The rain had stopped. She walked through the stretch of the flooded road, screaming out for Smriti again.

Her echoing voice numbed her mind, and the cold water numbed her body. She wept in the middle of the flooded road – destitute, frightened, and shattered. She scouted around, but no one was in the street.

She cried as she had nothing else to do, no way to help Smriti.

The police arrived at the site. They asked her where the exact spot of disappearance was. She led them to the manhole.

A man dived in and peered into the manhole.

Jia went under the water and saw the man-hole – open due to carelessness and irresponsibility. The polluted water had made her skin itchy and her eyes sore.

The man came back up. "No signs," he announced.

"Need a lady constable. Send a towel," the policeman ordered into his phone.

Jia stared into the streets – her heart, mind, and spirit were frigid. She stared into the obscurity of the moment. Time froze as she was washed over by the murkiest of nightmares. She could no longer feel her itchy skin and burning eyes, she could no longer hear her mother's scream for her, or the laugh of the mean girls from school.

The shivers across her spine had stopped. Her body halted into an infinite devastation as it succumbed to the sensation of defeat, the black blanket of death.

Her head shook from side to side, as a reflex, as she encapsulated the hollowness of the moment. The policewoman walked her out, covering her in a towel.

Nausea pushed its way deep into her gut, making her vomit the moment she reached the police car.

She rocked back and forth, back and forth.

The lady constable put her arm around Jia's shoulder and held Jia's hand with her other hand.

They reached the apartment.

"Where is your father?"

"I don't have one," Jia replied flatly.

"Grandparents? Relatives?"

"I have no one, please leave me alone now," Jia spoke in pauses. "Go find my mother. Please go, find, my, mother."

The lady dropped her number in case she needed help.

Jia went into the shower, washed off the filth of the street. Wrapping herself in a towel, she went back to her bedroom. She crashed into her bed, soaking the bedsheet. Her head hit the pillow.

"Mumma …" she whispered into the air, closing her teary eyes and thinking of Smriti's heartwarming smile.

She slept through the evening and night, waking up the following morning to the sound of her doorbell.

She looked around their shared bed – Smriti was not next to her. Her insides flipped.

Having slept in her wet towel, she was frosty. She hugged her knees, pressing them against her bare breasts. Her skin was bitter and her bones were prickly.

The doorbell rang again. There was movement outside the door.

"Ma'am, please open the door, otherwise we will have to break it. *Ma'am please darwaza kholiye* (open the door)" a man bellowed and followed it up with doorbells. Jia put on a loose T-shirt to cover her body and a pair of shorts that was within her reach. Her hair had dried through the night and was frizzy.

She opened the door. Two policemen and the lady constable stood at the doorstep.

"Yes?" she asked with her eyebrows raised, her voice supported by a looming hint of hope.

"Sorry," the policeman said, looking downward.

"You couldn't find her?" Jia asked. Her chest choked up; fear and anger took over every inch of her.

"We found her body, at the shore. Please come with us to claim it when you can. We will wait with you," the police stated solemnly.

As her brain registered the words, Jia slumped to the floor, unconscious. The lady constable rushed to care for her. She covered her in a blanket and lifted her onto the sofa of the living room. She rubbed Jia's soles.

When Jia opened her eyes, she clung on to the lady constable's lap. She hugged her and cried until she was interrupted by the policemen.

"Please get her dressed to come along with us," they suggested to the women.

Jia couldn't move. The lady constable changed her into a fresh set of clothes.

She had seen Smriti's body vanish into nowhere.

She closed her eyes. The vision seeped through her body. The policeman talked about her mother as a body. Their voice echoed in her veins, her flesh absorbing grief.

If only she had not pressed Smriti to take her to school that day. Jia retched, and guilt washed over her.

She got dressed. Cold and dazed.

She walked out of the house with the policemen as an orphan.

They took her to identify Smriti's recovered body. She looked at Smriti's pale face, touched her forehead, the ear piercing they had gotten together, the nose that she'd taken after, the lips that smiled with her through the worst times, the cheek she loved to kiss as a little girl. She grazed Smriti's features, her collarbone. A tornado of grief rose from the center of her stomach and froze her.

She wanted to leave the world with her mother.

"Mumma …" she let out a whisper, and then she cried. "Mumma …" she screamed at Smriti's frigid body. "Get up, Mumma."

The lady constable led her away.

"Mumma …" she yelled again, falling to the ground, holding her empty self from shattering into bits.

"I'll be alone now, Mumma, please … don't go … Mumma …" She broke into the longest, incontrollable howl.

She wailed, begging for death to take her, despising the universe for having saved her from her suicide attempt. She wept in the arms of no one, as the only one who loved her had left her side.

"Mumma, I'm homeless …" Jia cried, burying her face in her palms.

The control room resonated with her ripples of pain.

Policemen let silent tears out as they watched the sixteen-year-old grieve for her mother.

But no amount of empathy could make up for the sloppiness of the corporation due to which Smriti was no more.

"It is because of your fucked up system that this has happened," Jia yelled at them. "Because of your goddamned attitude."

She wanted to physically vent out her anger toward the system. She shivered with the need for it.

Jia needed to take care of her mother's rites. She knew nothing of it.

She relied upon the one friend her mum had – Lata.

She dialed Lata's number for help with the cremation. Lata could not believe her ears. Life was cruel to Smriti, but even tougher for Jia.

"I will arrange for everything; please do not worry about anything," Lata assured.

Lata and Mohit arranged for the cremation.

Jia watched the flames blaze her mother into ashes, as a moment of impossibility. In her pyre, bits and parts of Jia also blazed away.

The lit wood in her hand dropped, as the weight of death was heavy on her delicate shoulders.

"Please come and live with us," Lata urged after the rites were over. "I will come along to pack your belongings."

Jia did not answer. Who was she to contend her destiny anymore?

"Mohit, you'll have to pick Avantika from dadi's. Skip your tennis tournament. I have to be with Jia," Lata told Mohit.

Mohit nodded.

Lata and Jia entered the apartment. Jia sat in the corner of her living room. She could not look at the pictures that surrounded her.

Lata packed her bag silently. She placed her clothes, her school uniform, her shoes, and other belongings into a suitcase. She found thc stories written by Smriti and the sketches drawn by Jia.

Amazing, she thought to herself, and packed them in Jia's suitcase.

She came out to the living room where Jia was sitting. She picked up the photo-frames and placed them into the suitcase.

She saw a small clay lion-cum-fish in the living room, next to their photo-frames, and held it in her hand, wondering how Smriti and Jia were connected to Singapore. Jia watched as Lata scooped up the Merlion. She had never asked her mother where it came from. She nodded to Lata, agreeing to add it to her belongings.

Lata held Jia's hand and led her outside the apartment. The apartment that held Smriti's aura.

Lata pushed open the door to her apartment. Savitri didi, the house-help, ushered Jia's luggage into the guest room. It was a modest room compared to their handsome, modernly furnished apartment. The walls were painted white, the bed was upholstered with a peach fabric, and a small TV was displayed on the opposite wall.

"Do you want to eat something?" Lata asked Jia.

Jia shook her head and shut the room door after Lata and Savitri didi left. She lay on her bed and put on her usual hard rock.

I did meet Lata Aunty and her family on Sunday evening, Mummy, but without you … Jia reflected, and a blanket of ice spread across her chest. All the roses and greens present in her heart chakra got covered in frost.

***

A week passed. Jia had not spoken a word, had not unpacked her belongings, and lived out of her suitcase. Every time the memory of Smriti's drowning or cremation came up, she blocked it out. She diverted her mind to their memories or the lyrics of her music.

"*Jia ne kuch khaya hai subhe se?* (Has Jia eaten anything?)" Lata asked Savitri didi as she entered the house in the evening.

The house-help shook her head. "*Subhe se kamre mein hi hai. Lunch k liye bulaya tha par nahi aaye. Aap ek baar dekh lijiye.* (She's in her room since the morning. I called her for lunch, but she didn't respond. You may check once)."

"*Aap dinner lagao. Main bulaati hu* (You lay the dinner, I will call her)," Lata said, heading to Avantika's room to meet her.

Avantika was playing video games in her room.

"Hi beta, how was your day?" Lata paused her video games.

"My day was decent. You're late again! It is 8:00 p.m."

"I'm sorry. You know how demanding my work is," Lata excused herself.

"At least now you should be home timely. Jia didi is sad," Avantika said.

"Did you speak with her?" Lata asked, pulling her into a hug.

"No, she hasn't come out of her room," Avantika told Lata, hugging her back. "I feel bad for her, Mummy."

"Change into your night suit and come out for dinner; we'll knock on her room for dinner," Lata said.

"*What time will you be home?*" Lata texted Mohit.

"*I want to be out till late, anything urgent?*" Mohit texted back.

"*We should be having dinner with the kids,*" Lata texted.

"*Will try,*" Mohit's reply shot back.

Avantika and Lata sat for dinner. Lata knocked on Jia's door. Jia opened the door on the third knock, groggy and uncomfortable.

"Aunty, I don't feel like –"

Avantika cut her short, "Jia didi, please eat with us."

Jia regarded the chubby eleven-year-old wearing thick black spectacles, and a wide inviting smile, and nodded, taking a place at the table.

Lata and Avantika began eating. Jia nibbled on her meal and didn't speak a word. The dining table echoed with the clamor of the steel spoons and forks. She went into the room as soon as she was done. Her frozen heart was buried in a black box, away from any possible sunlight.

Mohit joined in after Jia had gotten up. He kissed Avantika on her head and sat at the dining table.

"Papa, Jia didi has already gotten up. Why can't you come early?" Avantika complained.

"Sorry beta, I was in a meeting," Mohit said, exchanging looks with Lata.

"You're lying, you were out with friends," Avantika cried. "Neither of you are home, you don't care."

"That's not true!" Lata said.

Mohit placed his hand on her thigh and shook his head.

"You both are involved in your own lives … you brought Jia didi home but don't take care of her!"

Lata rubbed her forehead. "We'll do more … promise."

"How was your day at school?" Mohit asked.

"It was okay. They've added new items in the canteen menu – hummus sandwich, pasta, and donuts. And the math teacher was absent, some substitution teacher had come. We watched a movie during class. Yutika had sneaked in her iPad to school …"

Lata and Mohit exchanged glances.

"What happens if you guys get caught?" Mohit asked.

"The iPad will go … she has spare ones at home so it's okay," Avantika explained casually.

Lata's face reddened; worry lines appeared on her forehead.

They chatted for a while longer.

Once they were in their rooms, Lata told Mohit, "We've to be home more."

"Jia will be okay, she needs time … It has been a week."

"No, not just for Jia, but for Avantika too. Whether she likes it or not, we have to monitor her … And for each other too. This week has made me realize how short and unpredictable life is. We used to be madly in love, Mohit. We were the couple that couldn't keep our hands off each other. And the picture-perfect family. What happened?"

"Life happens Lata, not just with us, with everyone. I have my work and friends, and you have yours, soon Avantika will have hers …" Mohit said, meeting Lata's eyes.

"I lost a friend, Mohit," Lata said, edgy. "I lost my best friend. I need you to be there for me …"

She cried. Mohit pulled her under his arm and kissed her forehead. "I'm sorry, I'm so sorry ..." he said, adding, "Yes, I'll be home … And the three of us will help Jia get better. I promise."

Lata nestled into him. He kissed her teary cheek and played with her hands. She placed her palm on his chest and kissed it.

***

A month passed. Jia bunked school and watched the clock tick through the day, staring into space or fiddling with the music on her phone, exploring newer artists in the same genre. She stayed in her room, until pulled out for dinner by Avantika. She ate enough to survive. Not because she wanted to survive. She had already failed at taking her life once. If she could, she would have taken her life again. But now she was too weak to want anything for herself, even death.

Lata knocked on Jia's room.

"Hi beta," she said, pushing her way into the guest room, "Savitri didi will take out your clothes from the suitcase and settle them in the closet, why don't you come sit with me?"

Jia shuffled out into the living area and sat beside Lata; her head lowered.

"You have to resume school, beta," Lata suggested to Jia.

"I don't care about school," Jia muttered under her breath.

Lata gave a moment's pause, thinking, *how do I do this? Smriti, you were the parenting expert …*

"Have you had lunch? Beta, you are getting weak, you have to come out of your room, go out in the sun," Lata said, almost scared of reaching out to Jia.

Jia did not reply. She kept her gaze lowered.

"What about therapy?" Lata asked, exasperated.

"If she's done settling the closets, I'd like to return to the room, please." Jia got up and left, going back to binge-listening her music.

"How can we be there for you?" Lata asked.

Jia said, "Don't. Don't be there for me. Leave me alone."

I do not care about stupid lunch or sunshine, or clothes in a closet, or school, or that damned therapy, Jia thought to herself, pulling her blanket over her head and going back to daydreaming about Smriti. She daydreamed of a happy house … the holiday by the beach from when she was nine, they had made jewelry with sea shells … the birthdays Smriti had celebrated for Jia, calling her intimate school friends, ordering a Barbie cake for her … the solace in Smriti's eyes when Jia was happy …

There, she could sense her mother's presence, see her mother's smile, eat her mother's rajma chawal. It was the only way she could live on – by still having a parent in her illusions.

Amidst the chaos that surrounded her, her mind offered her a heaven, and unmatched with the heavens above, to escape in dreams was real.

***

Two months passed. Jia had not attended school yet. Her dreams gave her a life she deSired – one with her mother. The difference between memories and illusions were blurring. Smriti's caring smile was engraved in her soul.

"We've to do something," Lata told Mohit. "We can't have a teenager sitting idly in her room listening to music, it is scaring me."

Mohit nodded. "We'll have to get a doctor home, if she doesn't come out. I'll speak with her during dinner."

During dinner, Mohit explained, "Jia, your mother was fiercely independent. She could manage you and herself for sixteen years. She had planned a life for you even after she left." He opened an envelope and showed her the life insurance check. He showed her the property papers of her ancestral property.

"We've created a bank account for you. We will sell your property and get the proceeds transferred to you once you turn eighteen. Smriti has made sure that you are covered through your education. Please do her efforts justice by going to school and taking care of yourself."

"I didn't know …you've been managing these things …" Jia studied the family whose house she was living in for two months. Being caught up in her darkness, she had not spared the verve to be grateful to them. "Thank you for everything."

"The loss of a parent is an endless battle, but come what may, your time is going to go on, Jia. You have the choice of spending it glorifying your mother's efforts and memories," Lata explained. Mohit held her hand under the table.

"I will go to school," Jia promised.

Avantika cheered excitedly, "Yay didi!"

Jia nodded and got up.

"Ek cup garam doodh andar dedo usko, (Give her a cup of warm milk in her room)" Mohit said to Savitri didi.

Jia noticed Savitri didi, her mehndi-dyed hair, her broken-tooth smile, her waist skinnier than the saree fabric draped around it. She took the *haldi* milk from her hand. Her head buzzed with the heavy metal she had been listening to all day.

As she sipped the warm turmeric milk sitting on her bed, listening to the sound of silence, a flash of realization ran through her – her mother was still looking after her.

***

Four months passed. Jia went to school. Even though she had taken a sensible step toward recovery, her mind was attuned to excessive daydreaming and her heart was still as stony as it could be. It was not going to be filled by a desire for a strong career. She had taken her baby steps into sunlight, but she still had the umbrella in her hand.

She dwelled in her bed, escaping into her parallel reality till the snoozed alarms gnawed at her brain. She then strolled through the school, forlorn, scribbling song lyrics in her notebook while the teachers lectured, heading back home, surviving on meager bites, and spending time with her hosts with her head lowered in gratitude.

She spoke little, even to her friend, Neena, who reached out to her.

One evening, during dinner, Avantika was throwing a tantrum.

"*Mujhe nahi khana hai roti sabji* (I don't want to have flat bread and vegetables). Mom, why don't you cook continental dinners like Yutika's mother!" Avantika hollered. "I'm ordering myself a burger. Jia didi, do you want one?"

Jia looked at her plate.

The sabji does suck, Jia thought, *Mummy made gobi (cauliflower) so well.*

She nodded.

Mohit ordered burgers for the kids.

"Papa, *waffle bhi kardo* (order waffles too)," Avantika whispered into Mohit's ear.

When Avantika dug into the burger, her eyes lit up. She finished her burger; Jia was halfway through.

"Today, our English teacher was late. So, everyone was loitering outside. And suddenly someone shouted, 'Ma'am is coming'. The class ran inside in a hurry, but this girl, she slipped on the floor. She fell on her bum, and she shouted, 'aiyooo' loudly. The entire class laughed. Ma'am kept saying, 'class shh, class sshh.' Nobody listened to her, and like that the bell rang. We didn't study the entire period," Avantika told the story, gesticulating. Her eyes widened with animation.

Jia chuckled, and then she smiled, understanding that Avantika was exaggerating the story for her. Her smile, akin to the smile of a newborn baby, was a moment of celebration.

Lata and Mohit watched from a distance, with relief. But the moment didn't last long.

Mohit laid Avantika's waffle on the table. Avantika's smile widened and she picked up her fork to dig in.

"Why couldn't we have ended on the burgers? Why do you need to have desserts after every meal, Avantika?" Lata chided.

"You just can't let me be, can you?" Avantika snapped, her fork mid-air.

"I care about your health, Avantika. Mohit, why did you order this for her without telling me?"

Mohit shrugged. "Let her eat."

"It is always a struggle. I won't even enjoy my dessert now," Avantika said, flipping her short hair with her hand in irritation. "You have a problem with your daughter being fat. That's all. You don't like how I look and can't show off to your friends."

"My God, the things in your head. No mother can dislike her child. When you'll be a mother, you'll understand me," Lata fought back. "Mohit, you have to help me here. Stop hogging yourself."

"Your mother loves you, Avantika," Mohit said, his mouth filled with waffles.

As Jia watched them bicker, her heart inched backward. She felt like an outsider in their family. She craved her own parent. She went back into her room, pulled her blanket over her head, and drifted into her dreams.

***

Six months passed. The music she listened to gave her absconding mind and stifled chest company. It resonated with her frequency and comforted her. This comfort was reliable. Metallica, Guns N' Roses and AC/DC had become her allies in numbness, just like her daydreams.

Jia had finished with her Class Eleven examinations and was promoted to Class Twelve.

One day, Avantika could not find her notebook, and she went into Jia's room to hunt for them. While looking for them, she came across the stories and drawings that Smriti and Jia had created.

She ran to Lata to show them to her.

"Yes, I've seen these," Lata said to Avantika.

"She should do something about it, no?" Avantika said.

When Jia came back home from school, Lata sat her down.

"You must continue this. It will be an outlet for you," Lata convinced the scrawny, eccentric, dazed girl sitting and nibbling on her lunch. "This might become something someday."

Jia protested, "I do not – I cannot do it without mom …"

"Please try … Smriti would have wanted you to …" Lata said. "I didn't know she wrote so well … Jia, if you plan on sketching further, I can scout for opportunities after school. Maybe as an illustrator."

"Thank you, I will let you know," Jia replied.

I'm not interested in opportunities, she thought.

She went to her room and glanced at the stories they had written together. It had been a while since she'd seen them. She read them to herself, reminiscing about how they had written them through the evenings of that one year during which she was healing.

She hugged the stories, and after six long months, she embraced her loss. "Mummy …" she whispered as she lowered her lids over brimming eyes.

Even those two dribs from her eyes made her heart lighter.

She went up to Avantika and asked her how her day was. Avantika, surprised that Jia had taken a step toward her, lurched herself at Jia and kissed her cheek.

"Come didi, I will show you my toys!" She pulled Jia into her room filled with toys and role-play set ups – doll houses, kitchen sets, doctor sets.

Jia spent an hour playing with Avantika.

On Lata's insistence, Jia went back to her therapist.

"Don't even try," she told the therapist, the moment she sat with her.

The therapist nodded.

"Do you want to listen to music together?" the therapist offered.

Jia nodded.

She introduced the therapist to her songs. "This is all the bond we're going to share, please." A year had passed. Jia religiously went to school, ate her meals, and spent time with her host family. For someone who had gone through a series of slumps, the routine was a rainbow.

Since Jia's boards were approaching, she studied through the day, and because Art was her fifth subject, she was sketching.

Mohit and Lata came home on time from work.

"Let's go for a movie on, Sunday," Mohit said.

"Movie! Movie!" Avantika cheered.

"Isn't it your colleague's birthday on Sunday?" Lata asked Mohit in a low volume.

"Won't go, let's spend it with the kids." Mohit exchanged a look with Lata. She placed her head on his shoulder.

Jia took a bite of methi parantha in her mouth. Her mind was still immune to taste.

"Avantika, go and finish your project then! You have to submit it on Monday," Lata said.

Avantika rolled her eyes and said, "*Bachao,* Papa.(Save me, Papa)." Mohit pouted.

"Savitri didi, *guest room se iska table le aao*. (Savitri, bring her table from the guest room)" Lata said.

Guest room, Jia thought, sighing. *Right, I am their guest.*

***

Eighteen months had passed. With her day dreams being her only distraction, Jia had studied adequately for her boards. She took her exams, fairly.

"What is it that you want to do after school, Jia?" Lata asked over dinner.

"Fine arts," Jia replied, talking in as few words as possible.

"The world is your oasis; you can apply to any college you want. The funds are secured," Mohit said.

Definitely not Mumbai, Jia contemplated, *I have to get away from here.*

Jia surfed colleges and applied to New Delhi, London, and a school in Singapore.

Irrespective of the fact that her efforts were half-hearted, she excelled in fine arts. The pain she had suffered had made her an easy artist. A simple swish of her painting brush conveyed more than she intended.

Jia got through a college in New Delhi and the one she had applied to in Singapore.

"Go to Delhi, you'll be closer to us," Lata persisted. "It'll be accessible for us to visit you often."

"No! Go to Singapore, didi! You will get to explore more!" Avantika shrieked with excitement. She was right of course. Jia would get to explore another country by going to Singapore.

Jia Googled Singapore and one of the images she saw was of the Merlion – the lion-cum-fish statue. She rushed to her belongings and compared the tiny sculpture she had picked up from their living room. Though it was a rougher version, there was an uncanny resemblance to the Merlion from Singapore. She wondered how her mother was connected to the foreign land.

If her mother had still been around, Jia would have continued staying in Mumbai.

Where are you, Mumma? You have forgotten your promise, left me alone, Jia sketched roughly as she thought.

Her heart was weak. Her boarding school days scared her. She did not want to do it again.

Even if Lata's home was another family's home, it was still comfort. Even though it was not the protection of her mother, it was still her mother's chosen people.

Jia stayed in bed till she could. Until the realities of life dawned on her – she had to get up and go to college irrespective of how she felt about it. She had grown affectionate toward Avantika. Her hyper energies and food-tinted glasses for life, had made Jia smile.

Jia remembered Smriti's words. *At a crossroads, choose what makes you feel lighter, what detangles.*

"Okay, I will choose Singapore then," she stated, giving Avantika the thrill she was longing for. Avantika sprang up in the air. She threw her arms and stifled Jia in a tight hug.

"Will you come visit me?" Jia asked her, her eyes showing a rare glint.

"I will, didi! I will come to study with you! But you will have passed out by then, no? Didi, how old are you? Do you know I will be thirteen soon!" Avantika yakked on.

***

Soon it was time for Jia to leave for college. Luckily, she had gotten a spot in the college hostel.

She visited the apartment that was left unadministered after Smriti's demise. She had grown up there. She recalled leaving for the boarding school – with mixed feelings, excitement, and sorrow as she was leaving Smriti alone in the space. She was worried about Smriti when she had not called, thinking of what could have gone wrong in this very apartment. She remembered the police informing her about her mother's body.

She shivered. She packed the things she needed, and looking at Lata, she whispered like a ghost, "Aunty, you can get it cleaned. Take care of it for me, please. I don't want anything to do with it. Please put it on sale."

Jia was quiet for the remainder of her stay.

She bid farewell to this God-sent family of three and thanked them endlessly with her heart. They bid farewell to the teenager who had reconnected them again. Project Jia had got their family close.

I am an orphan … I am alone in the world … The thought did not scare her, but it made her mature beyond measure.

She headed out, with her suitcase, her art portfolio, her cell phone, her bank details, and an unknown resilience. She had survived for a year without her mother and was still breathing. What else could go wrong in her life? What else could she be made to face that she could not bear?

The curly-haired Jia stood taciturnly at the check-in counter. Her phone's wallpaper was a picture with Avantika now. They had taken it when, Avantika was trying to feed her pancakes. Avantika's zeal had made her smile and pressed her for a selfie.

She sat in the waiting lounge, ready to board, with her earphones blaring metal music. She surfed through the newspapers and magazines that were sprayed across the waiting lounge. A magazine with a man's solo portrait on its cover stood out amongst the lot. The man, in his mid-forties, had a hairline that stretched backward to show the beginning of balding. A broad smile filled with genuineness, his nose crooked from the center, brown almond-shaped eyes radiating warmth, struck a chord within her.

She took out her paper and sketched his face with her pencils.

"Chopra's 101 on the Start-Up Ecosystem," the cover said.

An ordinary brown-skinned man, who had made it big in the international start-up ecosystem. Jia hmm-ed to herself. Had she been her ordinary self, she would have been impressed. But for now, she was a hollow cast and nothing moved her.

Sketching his portrait helped her kill time. They announced the departure of her flight, and in she went, at the nudge of a thirteen-year-old, on a voyage away from her past, and into another life.

CHAPTER EIGHT

Walk the road ahead with faith
If it showers
The universe will send an umbrella
Or it'll play a song to dance to

THE FIRST BREATH that Jia took outside the Singapore Changi Airport flushed her. It was hotter than Mumbai. The afternoon view of manmade structures and hints of nature – the layers of flyovers, the openness of the roads, the height of the buildings, the bustling roadsides and green pathways, the clear sunny sky, the variety of Asians, the polite taxi driver – was spewed with discipline.

Jia checked into her twin-sharing hostel bedroom, anxious about who her roommate would be. She settled her things into her closet, hitting the bed with her music blaring on speakers instead of earphones. She placed Smriti's stories and her sketches next to her portfolio in an accessible glass drawer, with her sketching tools.

She took out the caricature she had drawn in the airport and stuffed it in the middle of her portfolio. After lying down for a while, she was hungry. She walked across her hostel, asking the matron where the canteen was, and bought herself a plate of vegetable fried rice.

A few girls sitting at a table next to hers were joking and laughing. Jia was cautious of schoolmates now – especially groups that jeered. She continued to eat, appreciating the flavor of the food.

When she went back to her room, she saw that her roommate had checked in. She peered from the shy opening of the door to prepare herself for what lay ahead. For fair reason, she was anxious about whom she had to live with. The glint of flush on her cheeks from when she landed in Singapore vanished as she stood outside her door trying to take note of her roommate. Jia had left her music on. Her spirits were lower now than they had been when she had gone to the boarding school.

She's going to hate my songs, she thought, *and me.*

She tip-toed toward her bed, trying to avoid any conversation with this girl, but it was in vain.

"OMG! You scared meeee!" came a shrill voice in a thick Chinese accent.

Hair fringed and chopped perfectly to land above her brow, wearing jeans that fit snugly on her skinny legs, narrow shoulders peeping from a cold-shoulder top, and skinnier than Jia, a worried Chung pranced as Jia entered her room like a thief.

Jia met her gaze. She was more overwhelmed than Jia. Jia smiled to calm her down, stepping out of her whirlpool of emotions to recognize another's.

"You scared me! Why are you coming inside like a thief?" Chung said. "Aren't you my roommate? So, this is your room too!"

Jia nodded. Chung relaxed her shoulders.

"My name is Ai Chung. You can call me Chung. What is yoursss?" she sang as she extended her hand toward Jia.

"Jia," Jia stated in her highest volume, which was still a whisper.

"Are you here to study art?" she asked her, looking at the glass drawer filled with art tools.

"Yes, fine arts," Jia replied. "And you?" she asked her politely.

"Entrepreneurship and management," Chung replied, her chin lifted up. Jia noticed the pile of books, lying on Chung's bed.

"Have you already read these?" Jia asked, squinting her eyes and tilting her head.

"Where ar' you f'om? Where do you' parents leeve?" Chung asked in her Chinese accent.

"I am from India, Mumbai." Jia ignored the question about her parents. "How about you?"

"China, o' course!" Chung replied.

"Do you mind my music?" Jia asked, holding her breath.

"I liked it. It is not what I usually listen to, loud but differen'. I will study after freshening up, maybe that time you can put it off," Chung replied, surprising Jia at the studying part, yet not enough to invite conversation.

"Perfect." Jia sighed with relief.

She continued with her day, taking out her drawing sheet and scrubbing her pencils across the sheets in an ad-hoc abstract manner. She gazed out from the small window that was positioned between their two beds and waited for time to pass. Judas Priest's "Breaking the Law" filled the silence between them.

Chung quietly finished her "settling in" and sat to study. Her book had the name *Impress the Investor* spelled out on its cover.

Jia's otherwise dazed mind caught the name on the book Chung was reading.

The name "Keshav Chopra" was printed below the title.

Chopra.

She had read that name somewhere.

"Can I see that book for a second?" Jia requested.

She touched the embedded name.

Is this the man whose caricature I drew at the airport? He is mentioned for the same topic, Jia thought. *Could be, how does it matter …*

She returned the book to Chung without checking the caricature.

As the night turned, Jia covered her head under her blanket and drifted to her memories of Smriti.

College commenced the following day. Jia strolled to her designated classroom, observing the campus around her. She was going to spend three years there. The fine arts classroom was a cylindrical hall made of wood; the roof was a tinted fiber-glass sheet which welcomed sunlight. Planters were placed all over. The natural elements together made the hall a warm environment to create art in.

She scouted around her classroom. Kids from various countries were hustling and familiarizing themselves. They were tied by one strong trait – creativity. In an uncanny way, Jia was surrounded by more people like her. She fit in.

After introductions and customaries, Jia's first class was an empty canvas, an invitation to paint a fresh life. She painted a lady running into the woods. Wind blew through her wavy hair and her buttercream flowy dress. Her bare feet pranced along buds and weeds, and the forest's shadows bounced off her shoulders.

The teacher analyzed each of their paintings.

"Where is she going?" she asked Jia.

"Into a familiar world," Jia replied, closing her eyes.

"And what does she want to leave behind?" the teacher asked.

"Herself," Jia said.

"So, she doesn't know herself?"

"Yes, and she wants to run away from that unfamiliarity. Into a familiar world ..."

The teacher placed her hand on Jia's head.

The professors explained the structure of the course – history of fine arts and the works of famous artists, landscape painting, still life painting, cartooning, and so forth. Jia enjoyed the lectures. There were no signs of bullies, no heavy studying that she could not cope with, and no time to live in the clouds. Not used to concentrating, she was exhausted by the end of college hours.

She headed back to her hostel in silence. Chung was already there, studying.

"How was your day?" Jia asked, placing her bag on her study table, and taking off her shoes.

"There is so much competition. In China's schools only Chinese, and then also I never came first – top ten but not first; and here students are from everywhere. And everyone is good in Business Studies. Everyone will compete for those limited jobs," Chung whimpered, looking up from her book.

"First day of college and you're already thinking of a job!" Jia said, amused.

"What else, don't you think of job?" Chung asked.

"No, if I think of anything, it is either art or music," Jia said.

"Wow, your parents must be relaxed …" Chung said.

"Yeah, they are …" Jia said. "So, you're studying, that means I have to put my music on earphones?"

"Uh-un." Chung nodded.

Jia put music on her earphones. She scrolled through her playlist and scouted for the right song.

Aah, this is relaxing, she thought, closing her eyes. She placed one hand over another and tapped her fingers.

Chung took out some snacks to munch on.

"Would you like to try some?" she asked. "Would you like to try some?" she asked loudly again, and then shook Jia from her trance.

Jia took her earphones off and took the packet in her hand. The packet had white squishy rings with some powder. "What are these?" She fiddled with the pack. "It looks interesting."

She picked out one in her hand, put her finger through it. Finding it fascinating, she picked out five rings and put them in five fingers. It reminded her of a school snack, Crax.

Jia was about to place them in her mouth when –

"Squid rings," Chung said.

"What?"

"Squid – seafood?"

Jia shook her hand vigorously. The rings fell off her. "Eww. I'm vegetarian."

"Ohh … so you can't have these," Chung said, "I have pork, beef, fish candy … you can't have any of those!"

Jia stared at her wide-eyed, and handed the packet back to Chung.

Chung placed a piece of squid in her mouth.

"Squid is my favourite. They bring the brine out perfectly. Oh wait I do've seaweed tchoo," Chung said through her filled mouth.

"What's that?" Jia asked, the blank look on her face continuing.

"Weeds from the sea. Vegetarian, here try it." Chung handed her the roasted seaweed sheet.

"*Chhhi!*" Jia cried, taking a bite.

"You didn't like it?"

Jia sniggered. "Chung … you should discard the box."

"That is so rude, Jia. I would not say that about Indian food," Chung said.

Jia grinned and took another one from the box. "No, I'm joking, I liked it …"

She squeezed her eyes as she placed the seaweed strip on her tongue.

"You did? Wow. Have the full thing then." Chung passed the box to her. "I have my meat ones."

Jia muffled a laugh, fiddling with the box of seaweed.

She's so sweet, Jia thought, *how will I finish the box, I can barely take another bite.*

***

Weeks passed uneventfully. Apart from Chung, Jia didn't make friends in school. She went to school, undertook her art religiously, joined those around her for group assignments, and got out of school to head to her hostel. She conversed with Chung at bedtime. Chung was chatty, and Jia needed that much socializing.

They had simple conversations about their routines, cultures, and meals.

"I want to get a job in the USA and take my parents along with me. Their life in China has been irritating with our nosy relatives. I'm an only child. I want to give them a relaxed environment," Chung vented, opening her books.

"Where in the States would you settle down?" Jia asked, dreamily.

"I have a cousin in Texas. But I think Boston. I recently read a book that made me like Boston. It researched about it. It has a good work-life balance. New York is hustle-bustle," Chung replied with her chin lifted up.

Jia chuckled at the work-life balance comment.

"You are studying round the clock right now to have a work-life balance someday in the future. Is it not ironical?" Jia told her.

"Nothing in life comes easy; everything must be worked for, Jia. Why do you not know that?" Chung asked her with a frown, trying to talk some material wisdom into her. "You have to stop being so whimsical."

"I will visit you in Boston someday," Jia said and put her earphones on.

The conversation reminded her about her mother's letter from when she had asked her about the purpose of life. *"Take one day at a time, look for purpose in moments, not in the entirety of it."* She dug out the letters she had kept with her art portfolio.

She read one of her initial letters from Smriti.

Hello Jia,

I hope you are doing well my child. I read your letter. Though it gives me a faint idea of your dormitory and your classes, I still wonder how you are settling in.

I know you have coolers; do you need air conditioners? You are given meals at intervals, when you were here you could eat anytime you wanted, I hope you do not get hungry. What is your canteen like? When I come for the annual function, we can get your favorites from the canteen together. We can even explore some Indore specials.

I hope the people around you are nice. They come from diverse backgrounds, so they could be different than you. Try to look at the best in others.

Do enjoy your games and your arts.

You know, I got a promotion in office recently. Though I have always found my job boring, I am enjoying the seniority.

I love you more with each passing day.

Smriti

Jia sighed. She saw the Mufasa quote about how she should not go looking for troubles.

Maybe Srishti's mom gave her similar advice, Jia reflected.

***

She telephoned Lata and Avantika fortnightly.

"Please tell her to reduce her sugar intake, she listens to you," Lata told Jia over the phone.

"Don't eat sweets, you'll become *motu raam*, Avu," Jia joked with Avantika.

"Didi, leave this, tell me about Singapore *na* ..." Avantika's bubbly voice warmed her heart.

"Well, I haven't seen much. I enjoy my arts class. That's all. You come here for your college. We will explore Singapore together!" Jia replied in her meek voice, having little to tell Avantika. "My roommate is Chinese, and she has given me a box of seaweed to have."

"Oh didi, see I told you that you'd get to explore! Please go out of your hostel and see the city! My friends till me it is LIT," Avantika said. "I will make a best-things-to-do-in-Singapore list by reading travel blogs and email it to you."

"Wow, thank you! That is very sweet, Avantika."

"Whenever you miss Smriti, call me …" Lata told Jia.

Whenever I miss Smriti? Jia thought. *How can there be a minute when I do not miss her?*

"Sure, Lata Aunty, thank you …" Jia replied and wound up the conversations quickly. She curled up in bed, hugging her knees and going back to memories of Smriti. Hours passed in illusions.

In one illusion, Smriti was an old woman, and Jia was forty. They were sipping hot coffee by a waterfall and talking about life.

In another, Smriti was in her thirties, and Jia was eight. And they were watching a film together, sharing popcorn.

***

Living a life of routine, four months passed in Singapore.

Though Jia became accustomed to her routine, she was emotionally disconnected, living on because she had to, afraid of talking, of jinxing her life of stability. She was afraid of happiness. The last time she had felt an iota of joy, she had lost her mother.

Shade was alright – a little cold, but alright.

But while the universe can have its arduous monochromatic strains on life, it is also responsible for bringing streaks of quaint shades and animation. It seemed like the universe did not agree with trapping this artistic, eccentric, curly-haired dreamer in a twister of anesthesia.

It was time to shake her up, to open the boxes she had imprisoned her pain in. It was time that Jia was given a space to unleash her tears, feel her pain and heal it, so she could become the art that she was meant to be.

Chung was working hard to improve her scores in college. She went from reading one fat book to another, underlining and making notes through the hours. Jia's brain did not register the salary figures Chung wanted to draw after college. *What good would money do to anyone in this otherwise cruel world?*

One Sunday, when Jia was spending her usual hours in bed, with her eyes shut, daydreaming, Chung shook her.

"How do you do this? Spend the entire evening in bed? And on weekends you're spending two continuous days in bed. You listen to the same music again and again? Don't you get bored? Why don't you read a book or watch films?" Chung asked.

"I watch films in my head, Chung," Jia said in a mild tone. "It is enough entertainment for me. Please don't disturb me."

Chung blinked rapidly. "I worry," she murmured.

"Don't worry about me, Chung. I am okay …" Jia said. "Go back to your books, Chung."

"Yeah, you listen to your songs," Chung replied, scribbling notes.

That night after dinner, Jia told Chung that she did not have parents. She closed her eyes and confessed, "My father was never a part of my life. My mother raised me alone, and she passed away two years back. I am alone in this world."

Chung gasped.

"Sorry," she whispered as her eyes beaded with tears. "Jia …" she asked in a murmur, "when you keep your eyes closed, do you see your Mumma?"

Jia nodded, and breathing heavily, she added, "Yes, and sometimes … a full family … a father too … he doesn't have a face … but I see him."

Chung bit her quivering lip.

"Do you have grandparents?"

"My grandparents didn't accept my mother and me. I spoke with my grandmother sometimes, but my grandfather, not at all. They both passed away while I was growing up. In fact Chung, I can't recall what my *nani* looked like … She was nice."

"Why don't you try sketching your grandmumma?" Chung suggested.

Jia nodded, shifting from the bed to take out her art tools.

"Tell me about your mom," Chung asked. "How was she as a person?"

"My mom … she was peaceful … dedicated, neat … while growing up I remember she was fashionable, but by the time I was in my teens, she would wear simple kurta pajamas every day. She liked boring romantic music. My mother was simple."

***

"Simple, kind, and genuine, there is no one like Smriti," Keshav told Mahesh on the phone.

"Bhai, it's been three years since she left, it's time you moved on," Mahesh said.

"I fell in love with her. How often does that happen?" Keshav explained. "Is anyone in touch with her? How is she doing?"

"No idea bro, nobody was in touch with her. She quit abruptly, just dropped a text to Samir," Mahesh told Keshav.

"Yeah, left me abruptly too. Got her daughter back from boarding school … after that she cut contact."

I don't know why we broke up … Keshav thought for the hundredth time.

"Well, I have something to share with you," Mahesh said. "I am seeing someone."

"Wow! Mahesh, whom?" Keshav asked. "Is she from the support group?"

"No, I met her through an app. It has been two months. Man, life is good. I found Yashna. Divorce case is settled, Ishita is out of my life. I do have to talk to her about the kids though," Mahesh said.

"Yeah. Like I have to speak with Neha. I'm sure she feels similarly toward me," Keshav replied.

"How is Kaveer?" Mahesh asked.

"He is good; he was here for the summer. He got admission in Bangalore, has taken up engineering … full Mumma's boy!"

"It's because you let him be a Mumma's boy! You've got no fight in you." Mahesh sniggered.

"I'm good not fighting with anyone," Keshav said. "Anyway, why don't you and Yashna come by to Singapore sometime?"

"I will plan, for sure," Mahesh said.

"Mr Chopra, we'll have your speech now," a lady's voice tore their conversation.

"Uh Mahesh, I got to –" Keshav spoke.

"Yes, go on, I know you have work. Miss you bro. Find yourself a date … or a family, if that's what want. Smriti isn't coming back. If she had to, she would have by now."

"Yes." Keshav smiled.

If she had to, she would have … He let the words sink in.

He gripped his file tightly in his hand, took a deep breath, and walked toward a massive wooden door. An auditorium filled with young adults awaited him. He had been invited as a chief guest to a business school in Hong Kong.

***

"Monee is impo'tan', Jia. You need to concentrat'e on building a careeeer out of wha' you are doing, you know." Chung's chest boomed with conviction. Her beady eyes were filled with care.

"It is not important to me. I wonder what the fuss is about, you know … Everything works out eventually if it must and no matter what," Jia replied to credit the amount of effort Chung put in explaining things to her. She buried her head into her squishy pillow, closing her eyes and reconnecting with the music she had last heard in the morning while getting dressed for college.

"You yourself told me that your mother had to work hard to put you through school," Chung chided her.

"And see what happened – she left money and me, both, behind." Jia rolled her expressive eyes away from Chung. One part of her was dying to vent, and another part of her wanted to shut out any conversations about Smriti.

The side of her that did not want to vent won again.

"If she had left you with no monee, what would you have done?" Chung was realistic.

"Well, if Mummy would have left me penniless, I would have found you Chung!" Jia winked. She covered her head with her blanket.

I'm done Chung, don't talk about these practical things anymore, Jia thought to herself. *Please let me be.*

"Very funny, Jia. You need to get perspective. We have about two years in school, and then we must set our careers. By the way, you know Jia, by this semester's end, I need to come up with a start-up idea. If it is worth it, they will find me an investor – can you imagine, having my start-up while in school!" Chung explained.

"But don't you want to do a job?" Jia asked, tilting her head.

"I do, but Jia, it will be a great addition to my CV. And, I will get to meet such amazing people. I could be mentored by Keshav Chopra – he is the GOD of Southeast Asia's start-up ecosystem!" Chung said in her squeaky voice.

"Keshav Chopra – Chopra … where have I heard his name? He is the one that wrote your book, right?" Jia recalled seeing the name on Chung's textbook.

"Yes, yes! He is brilliant. It is a privilege to hear him talk even once in your lifetime. In fact, you should sign up when he comes to university! I will tell you whenever they have his seminar or talk planned. You must hear him talk Jia … what an inspiration!" Chung was awestruck by Keshav Chopra.

"I am not interested in business! You should know that by now," Jia replied in a flat tone.

"Then come because they say that he is inspiring, and he is Indian!! A brilliant Indian man – that should pull you out of your loud music for a while?" Chung giggled.

"Yeah sure." Then she remembered the caricature she had drawn in the airport. It had been buried for a while in the drawer where her mother's stories and her drawings were kept. She pulled it out. "Is this him?"

"Yes, of course! How did you draw a sketch of him if you never saw him?" Chung asked.

"I saw him in a magazine. I was bored so I copied his picture. He seemed, oddly interesting." Jia's tone turned softer, like she was talking to herself, as she wondered what had drawn her enough to sketch him.

"He is charming enough for anyone to want to sketch him!" Chung giggled again.

"He is an Indian uncle, Chung!" Jia laughed.

"You wait till you see him speak. I have heard some of his speeches on YouTube. Here, you should try listening to him." She offered her earphones.

"No, thank you," Jia replied with a smile, putting on her own earphones instead.

Chung motioned her to take off her earphones. "Listen, I am hungry, do you want to grab dinner?"

Jia nodded.

They entered the mess. The fragrance of fried food and the clatter of chatty students filled them up. Jia lined up for Indian meal and Chung helped herself to a pile of seafood chao fan and chicken mei fun.

"The chao fan here is better than in China!" Chung claimed as she devoured her meal. "Do you want to try?"

Jia shook her head, eating parantha and palak paneer.

Now I miss Lata Aunty's home food, Jia thought.

***

Two months later, when Jia came back to the room from school, she found Chung sobbing under her blanket. Chung was often stressed about her studies, chanting prayers before tests, or talking to her mother on the phone, but this was unexpected.

Jia noted the pile of books she had over her study table and thought, *she works too hard.*

"Hey, what happened Chungi?" she said, pulling her blanket off.

"I have to – submit – my start-up – idea tomorrow," Chung splattered one word at a time. She made eye contact with Jia. "Remember I told you? They are going to choose the top few for investment. I have scratched out my list. I have nothing to show them. What are my teachers going to think of me?"

"Okay, that's a small problem." Jia smiled, putting her arm across her shoulder. "Please stop crying, Chung," Jia said gently, amazed at her empathetic capabilities. She gave Chung a hug!

"Help me … please."

How can I help her, Jia contemplated.

She swirled Chung's pen in her fingers.

"Okay, listen. I do have something that can help you. It is personal though." Jia stretched toward the drawer she had stored Smriti's stories in. With quivering hands, she handed them to Chung.

"These go along with these artworks … see if you can use them …" Jia handed the stories and cartoons to Chung.

"What are these, Jia?" Chung asked.

"My mom used to write stories for children, and I used to sketch with her. It is a collection. Different themes have been covered – plants and animals, school, growing up, enchantments, magic, etc. They are value-system based fun stories. A lot of them were stories she told me as a child," Jia explained.

"Oh, wow!" Chung went through them. "You're so talented!" she said, surprised.

Jia touched them with a sigh, reminiscing the last memory of them sketching together.

Smriti was cooking in the kitchen. Though she had perfected her recipes over time, she loved to measure her ingredients before adding them in. She also kept washing her hands while cooking.

Jia had asked Smriti if she had met someone. Smriti had replied "maybe in a dream", and Jia had twigged the undertone. She had smiled to herself, understanding that even if her mother had a special friend, she had decided to keep it at bay for her welfare.

Now, recalling it, she realized – if this man did exist – there was a big chance that he did not know about Smriti's demise! Nobody had come for the funeral!

How had she not thought of this before? How had she not played the conversation in her mind earlier? Who was the person? And what about Tushar?

I wonder if Tushar knows, I wonder if he even cares.

"I doubt they know," she thought out loud.

"What are you saying? Who knows what?" Chung slit through Jia's trance. "Listen no … listen no …" She patted Jia's shoulders to bring her back to their room. "This is beautiful. But I cannot use it, Jia! It is your mother's work, her dream!" Chung flipped through the stories and the artwork.

"Use it. I won't do anything about it by myself," Jia murmured, her mind still on the men in Smriti's life.

"Someone could be that giving …" Chung looked into Jia's eyes, trying to figure out where this endless compassion came from. She fiddled with Jia's fingers. The artist sitting by her was broken, yet the most beautiful human being she had met. "Can you be a co-founder of my start-up at least?"

"No, no … this business is not my cup of tea, Chung." Jia shook her head.

"Listen, I won't do this without you!" Chung pressed, her eyes shining with honesty. "Please, Jia, wait what's your full name?"

"Jia Jain." Jia smiled.

"Wow, those are almost identical alphabets! Okay, Jia Jain, will you be my co-founder?" Chung proposed with hope in her eyes.

"No, no," Jia replied, shaking her head again.

"Please please," Chung begged, "I won't do it without you!"

"Okay, if you need me to be, I will be. Now, please smile, Ai Chung," Jia full-named her back.

Chung leaped on Jia and hugged her tight. They snuggled into bed together, turning one page after another, reading Smriti's stories and matching them to Jia's sketches. They became co-founders of their start-up – Mumsaga.

Chung's body touched Jia's underneath the quilt, and a strange tingling sensation ran through Jia. Chung continued to play with Jia's fingers. Jia looked at their fingers intertwined together, but she could not withdraw them even though she was uncomfortable. The impact of another girl's proximity … Jia held on to her heavy breath to not intimidate Chung. She hushed her racing heart.

She was taken back to Tanya – the senior whose smile had made her stomach flip. She had barely observed Tanya for a week when a bully of her school noticed the gaze and spread word that she was a lesbian. Before Jia could figure it out for herself, the school was buzzing with the news. In no time, her friends had deserted her. The word "lesbian" and the sharp tones of laughter had rung in her ears till she had broken down.

This had jeopardized her life in school. This attraction. It scared her now. She got angry at herself. She pulled back and excused herself, sleeping on her own bed.

She could not tell Smriti or her counsellor that this was the reason she got bullied. Now the pain of bullying or possibly being a lesbian, seemed petty when compared to the pain of being alone in the world.

She opened her eyes and glared at Chung. She had slept quickly.

She thought about the comfort her companionship had offered to her … The devil that made her skin tingle when she lay next to Chung … The devil that was going to ruin their friendship.

Don't think of her like that, please … nip it in the bud, she told herself, before closing her eyes and falling asleep too.

***

Forty student-preneurs pitched their work to a bench of senior professors at the University. The bench was to select five of them for mentorship and incubation.

Chung and Jia sat at their assigned desk together. Chung had prepared her idea pitch for Mumsaga and created a venture on paper.

She revised the presentation.

Jia rubbed her nails. Her most personal bond and precious memories were being unveiled in public. Was she ready for it?

Chung was called on to present details of their idea. With Smriti's storytelling, Jia's artwork, and Chung's business knowledge, Mumsaga was an interesting start-up.

Jia closed her eyes as Chung presented.

"I want to go back to the room. I am uncomfortable," Jia muttered, shaking her head, envisioning Smriti's kind face, envisioning Smriti writing the stories.

Nervously, they waited for the list of selections.

Without any impediment, they were chosen for incubation. "…and Ai Chung and Jia Jain for Mumsaga: Stories for Children," read the professor from the list of chosen start-ups.

"It's time to be allotted mentors now, Jia." Chung tugged at Jia's shirt and crossed her fingers.

"This is not cool, it's too much for me," Jia muttered anxiously.

Chung held Jia's hand. "Don't worry, Jia. Everything is going well!"

"Mumsaga will be mentored by Keshav Chopra," the professor's voice rang.

Chung shrieked, wept tears of happiness, and hugged Jia.

"You made it possible Jia, thank you!" Chung squealed.

"Keshav Chopra," Jia said out loud, "you must be so happy you got him."

"Yes, and I cannot wait for you to meet him," Chung said, spewing words out with speed.

"I'M GOING TO BE MENTORED BY KESHAV SIR HIMSELF!" Chung texted her mother.

Whether it was Chung's excitement rubbing off on her, or her tug toward this intriguing person now, Jia's anxiety calmed for a minute. Her head throbbed lesser. Though the display of their private bond in public was discomforting, she was calmed by the distraction.

An off-beat inclination lit a tiny firefly in her insides – the desire to meet this glorified man, Keshav Chopra.

CHAPTER NINE

The pigment shows color
Only when light is thrown upon it
The pigment is yours to create
The light is the universe's

WITH THE DISCUSSIONS of Mumsaga between the two of them, life became lively.

"Finally, tomorrow! Our first mentorship lesson with Keshav Sir. He will be addressing everyone first. Then we will have our hour with him. Jia, aren't you excited? Your own start-up! Your mother's voice and your sketches."

"Excited. Chung, Jia no do excitement," Jia replied.

She brushed through the pages of the story.

There was a story about how the fishes in the sea made a car with plastic to travel from one coral reef to another. Jia read it again, to absorb her mother's virtuousness – the bubbly manner in which she had fabricated and explained the environmental impact of plastic dumped into the oceans.

The mentorship would take place in the late afternoons after class hours. Jia would be free from her art lectures by then and Chung would be free from her business lectures. They could work on their start-up along with their mentor.

On the day of mentorship, Jia woke up confused about what she was doing. Her mind questioned what she wanted from this. She was overwhelmed by the mixed emotions of releasing her personal bond and the last memories with her mother, of helping Chung, and of meeting this famous man, Keshav Chopra.

She dressed in a formal shirt and a pair of black pants.

"Do we need a tie as well?" she asked Chung.

"I will wear one," Chung replied. She applied hairspray on her hair to slick it backward and finished her face with powder.

Jia picked up a tie. "Naaah …"

The preliminary meeting of the Start-up Incubation Program was being held in a massive well-ventilated meeting room. The five start-up attendees were assigned desks and chairs.

A nameplate, with "Mumsaga" written on it, was placed on one of the desks. Chung was already making notes. No one was speaking on the podium yet. Jia walked in silently and took her place next to Chung.

"What are you scribbling, silly?" Jia asked with her soft smile.

"I must be prepared to talk to Keshav Sir. You should prepare too." Chung shuffled through the stories and gave it to Jia. "How are we going to market the start-up? What is your designation and what is mine? When will we register our company? What are the laws of registering a company in Singapore? Jia, we do not know anything!"

Chung's fringes bounced against her forehead as she shook her head in worry.

Jia, don't think about how cute she looks, Jia thought, *there's enough on your plate.*

"Yes, because we are eighteen. We are not supposed to know everything, Chungi! Now let them teach us. Stop being so paranoid," Jia pacified Chung's concerns.

"They're coming in!" Chung said, leaping off her seat.

Jia turned her head toward the door.

The mentors walked in. Everyone present in the room clapped. The mentors took their places on a panel. There were three of them, and Keshav was sitting in the center.

Tall, heavy-shouldered, with a belly that bulged inches farther than his chest, Keshav Chopra seemed … cheerful. His Indian-gold skin tone and sharp Punjabi features were magnified by the genuine smile he gave to those seated ahead of him. His hair was salt and pepper. He was dressed in a polo-neck T-shirt, jeans, and a belt that brought attention to his protruding belly.

Jia compared the sketch she had made to the man before her – no, she had not done justice to the kindness on his face. She had not captured his compassion and humility … his soft aura!

Such young minds, I'm lucky to be here, Keshav thought, looking around the room.

One after another, the mentors addressed the student-preneurs. While one spoke of problem solving, inculcating the start-up mentality, the second spoke of vision, strategy, and niche markets. When the mic was passed on to Keshav, the students hooted and cheered in anticipation of his speech.

Jia noticed that beside the list of achievements and success stories under his belt, he was modest. He cracked a joke or two about reaching the university, the driver of his car – irrelevant topics to comfort himself rather than his audience, before he talked about "how a start-up founder needs to be full of emotions to transfer his vision to the world …"

"Our time in life is limited. If we can spend it doing what we love, we are living our truth. There is nothing above and beyond living your passion. When we work with passion, the universe flows through us, it complements us and our endeavors. The greatest quality of an entrepreneur is the quality of his passion. Because an enterprise is an extension of the entrepreneur, it is he who is reflected in the work he does. Thus, a start-up founder should be passionate, even emotional. Now while that is the first step, this passion is only accepted by the world when it converts into value for them. The three of us mentors, will join hands with you to deliver what you love to do in a strategic manner, so that it creates value for the world. We will sharpen your efforts in such a manner that the world will welcome your product, your emotion, your truth, the material manifestation of your energy. Value is what remains, as footprint, long after we have left this world. We will help you there – in delivering your talent, interests, and passion as value to the world."

The room basked in Keshav's benevolent voice, before it broke into an applause. He handed over the mic to the professor who was facilitating the meeting and sat down in his place.

"That was Mr Chopra! His unmatched intelligence and clarity has held Singapore's start-up ecosystem in its place. After his corporate stint, Mr Chopra began with his own start-up. He went on to founding tens of them. Mr Chopra has been mentoring and guiding start-ups for years now. Mr Chopra, we are fortunate to have you amidst us today. Thank you for your time and efforts at Singapore University."

The professor then laid out the structure and schedule of the Incubation Program. "We will meet after six months for an investor meet to raise funding."

Every time Jia had heard someone speak of business, career, or work, she had only heard about earning money. Nobody had spoken about work in a heavenly manner.

Mummy had not enjoyed her job. This is what she enjoyed, these stories … Would Mumsaga be her footprint in the world? Jia thought. *These stories are an extension of Mummy. These were her thoughts, her words. And my artwork … This start-up is an extension of our bond. Our time together ... How had I not thought about this?*

Her frosted heart chakra stirred. She got goosebumps.

She was going to carry on her mother's footprints.

I need to work hard on this, Jia thought, clutching the stories tightly in her hand.

Her eyes welled up. Chung shook her from her thoughts and mouthed, "I told you, he is GOD."

Jia smiled at her friend's excitement.

The combined session went on for another hour, before the start-ups were assigned respective meeting rooms. Jia and Chung were scheduled to sit with Keshav in one of those meeting rooms.

Keshav looked at the young Mumsaga team standing before him. They were one-third his age and one-third his size.

Jia's eyes caught his attention. His stomach lumped up as his heart skipped a beat. He had seen that light before.

He shuffled a file from his right hand to the left and extended his hand, for them to take individually.

"Keshav," he said, beaming.

Chung shook his hand vigorously. She held it for longer than acceptable. Jia was edgy, and got the vibe that he was nervous too. The mutual edginess comforted her.

She slipped her hand – her bony fingers, sleek palm, cold from the nervousness and confusion, into his broad, warm, and heavy hand – it snugged up her core. Her chest stirred again; a fuzzy sensation lightened her insides. In that second, she knew she was meeting someone special.

"Jia," she murmured and smiled.

Keshav stared at her for a moment.

There is an uncanny similarity between her face and Smriti's. Something about their eyes are similar … not the color but something else … and then that nose … that is definitely like Smriti's.

Keshav realized it would be uncomfortable for her, so he broke contact.

My mind is tricking me again, Keshav reckoned. *Smriti, where are you? I am still looking for you …*

His smile was the perfect smokescreen to his lonely spirit.

Chung smiled back. Her beady eyes got tinier as she squinted through them.

"Before we commence with your mentorship, why don't you both tell me about yourselves? We have to work with one another for six months, it will be good to know about your backgrounds. Where you are from, education, and your vision … a little something about what you want to do after college is over," Keshav started the session.

Chung began chatting. "I will do my internship, take up a job, then an MBA, preferably from an Ivy League. Then I want to work in investment banking, then I think I would switch to managerial finance later on after I've made money. I want to learn about digital media, some short courses, and a third language that will help me in the US later on, preferably French. And –"

"Okay there … we have six months to do this," Keshav joked, taking to his comfortable self. "How about you?" he asked Jia, inquisitive about this teenager with unconventionality smeared across her face.

"I am from Mumbai, India. I am studying Art in the university here. I am not sure of my vision yet. Maybe I will take up a job somewhere, maybe I will stay in Singapore. I don't know yet, Sir. This start-up was Chung's idea. I do not know about the business or visionary aspect of things," she said honestly in a flat tone and low volume.

"That is okay. Let's see if by the end of the mentorship session you enjoy business. You must have worked on the art work here? Or the stories?" Keshav had enough experience to presume talent and creative streaks.

"Yes Sir, artwork," Jia said.

"What about the stories?" Keshav asked.

"Jia's late mother," Chung said out loud.

"Oh, I'm sorry," Keshav said. He realized that it was not the shape or color of her eyes that was like Smriti's; it was the melancholy in her eyes that was similar to the melancholy in Smriti's eyes. The eyes bore a reflection of a strong heart, a stagnated soul.

"I'm sorry." Keshav knew better than to probe into personal matters. "How do we plan on continuing the stories? They form the essence of the start-up." Then Keshav moved to the obvious question: "How would you make your start-up not an event but a going concern? This is a supply gap to be brainstormed upon."

"We can get someone else to write the stories? Someone who has studied literature?" Chung suggested.

"But how would you continue the essence that Jia's mom's stories have? How would you carry on the messages and ethos that are there in these stories?" Keshav asked.

The girls were quiet.

"Please tell us," Jia asked, her eyebrows raised. The curiosity stimulated her. "How can we continue with my mother's voice?"

This start-up must mean a great deal to her, Keshav thought to himself. *I have to do my best here.*

"Well, you can draw out the parameters and traits that are there in these stories on a product vision canvas or product vision board. By reading the stories, we can map out the messages, the moral values, the ethics, the kind of characters that Jia's mother used and create a training tool for whoever will join us to write the stories next. That way, we will have defined what Mumsaga stands for and it will be a going concern, meaning, it will live beyond its founders."

Chung's mouth dropped; Jia's eyes widened.

They continued the session in admiration of their mentor.

"Don't worry, the full session won't be as heavy. We'll focus on learning one concept a day and then take our time to absorb it. We'll keep taking breaks in the middle."

"Yes, we finished with our school lectures before coming here," Chung said. "We will get tired."

"Aah, Chung, you have a long way to go in your career, don't count the hours already!" Keshav teased.

"Oh no, Sir, she is going to study once she goes back to the hostel," Jia teased. "I'll have to listen to music on my earphones."

Keshav smiled.

"We'll focus on the product canvas, then move on to the varied aspects of the business model – revenue streams, key partners, and so forth."

Two hours flew by, filled with wisdom and chatter.

Jia went back to her room in wonder as to the brilliant person Keshav Chopra was. Everything they said about him was true. Of course, he was intelligent. That was a given. But his affectionate smile and constant need to make others comfortable were underrated. Nobody spoke about his sweet demeanor, his approachability for students – how easy it was to open up to him … even for a closed book like Jia.

And he had found a way to eternalize Smriti's voice!

Her perspective toward Mumsaga had changed. Though she had given the stories to Chung to help her, it truly was her mother's legacy.

She took out their notes from the session and read through them.

What is it that Mummy intended through these stories? Jia thought. She underlined and took notes.

Jia researched Keshav Chopra over the internet. Divorced, has a son – her heart sank. *He has a broken family,* she thought. She read his Wikipedia bio and saw a picture that was taken when he was younger. His hair was black but his smile was the same. The kindness in his eyes was consistent. His talks were enigmatic and filled with light.

He had written books, mentored start-ups, and invested in them. There were articles that spoke of his intelligence and his magical touch for a start-up's career.

"We are receiving special attention, Mummy," Jia whispered out loud.

***

The touch of your simplicity has pierced my heart forever … and now I bleed … to see you laugh at my jokes, to kiss your neck … and hold you in my arms … Where are you, my Remembrance? Keshav thought, looking at his picture with Smriti. They had only one. They had taken it on the night he had proposed to her. *I met someone who reminded me of you … That girl had something about her, a fighting spirit. In her teenage years she has created art worth creating a start-up over. Brilliant stuff.*

He called Kaveer up.

"How are you, beta?" Keshav asked Kaveer.

"I am okay, Papa. The weather and people in Bangalore are brilliant, but honestly science is hard. *Mujhse nahi ho raha* (I am unable to do it). Interest *bhi nahi hai* (I'm not interested also)."

"Change your stream then, beta. I left my corporate career for my start-up. And that's where I found growth. Because I enjoyed it myself. Through my experience with other start-ups I've understood that it is inner fulfillment that drives growth," Keshav said.

"I will have to skip a year. Who will talk to Mumma?" Kaveer asked.

"You will, Kav. You will stand up for what you believe and want to do. What is it that you want to do?"

"Political Science," Kaveer admitted. "I want to work for and with the society. Apply to TISS."

"There is nothing greater for a parent to hear," Keshav replied. "Talk to Neha, stand up for your choices. If you need my support I am here, but don't waste your time on something you don't want to do."

"Yes, Papa, miss you," Kaveer said and hung up.

***

Keshav mentored Jia and Chung for two hours every week.

"Have we worked on the product vision canvas?" Keshav asked.

Jia nodded. She had written down the characteristics of the characters her mother had used in the stories, the value system she proposed, and the kind of settings she used to describe in the stories.

"Honesty, respect, empathy, cooperation, equality," Keshav read out loud. "Excellent."

He read through the heartfelt stories and corroborated them with Jia's drawings. "Jia, though your drawings are excellent, you should look at them with a deeper perspective and try to highlight these hidden messages in your artwork. I see scope for further harmony between the two."

"I will, Sir, thank you," Jia replied.

"Chung, let's see you work on the revenue models. Where can we market Mumsaga?"

"Sir, in stores –" Chung began her breathless recitation.

"Aah – no, not now. Take a week to work on it," Keshav suggested. "You may start your research now."

When the session got heavy, Keshav joked in the middle.

"What did you girls eat for lunch today?" he asked casually. "Let me guess, fried rice?"

"Yes!" Chung laughed. "How did you know?"

"I've been in Singapore for decades. I am a Punjabi who has forgotten what aloo parantha and butter tastes like. I eat with chopsticks all day," Keshav conversed. "But the funniest part is at times I forget whether I've had my meal! Do you girls think I am keeping too busy? Or are these signs of dementia?"

"Dementia, Sir." Jia chuckled in response.

Keshav laughed.

Jia worked late into the night to improve her sketches and align them with the stories. She wrote down the emotions she needed to incorporate in the caricatures and added them to the product vision canvas. Though she was doing it for Smriti, it was healing her. Working gave her little time to daydream. It distracted her from her illusions and brought her out into reality.

"You are on fire, Jia," Chung said one day, looking at Jia's vision board.

"Show me the revenue model," Jia asked Chung. Chung handed over the document.

"Wow, Chungi. This is extensive," Jia said, reading the list of places they could market Mumsaga.

"I've never seen you so active or passionate about anything," Chung said.

Jia blushed. "I'm enjoying it. Thank you, Chung. It is all because of you."

"No Jia, it is all because of you. Now tell me, do you want more seaweed?" Chung asked as she opened another box. "It kind of grows on you, doesn't it?"

Jia laughed, took a sheet, and placed it in her mouth.

"Yeah, surprisingly, it does!"

"The Chinese grow on you," Chung remarked and fluttered her eyelashes.

Jia turned red.

***

"You're doing great work on this project, kid. I've noted the changes in the sketches. They align with the stories and I'm impressed," Keshav said to Jia in their next session.

"Chung, even your revenue ideas are great. We need to work on them with Jia now. Chung, you should target one age group first and then target the next. Please sort the stories and drawings as per age group. Jia, can you modify the vision board to suit separate age groups? You will need to do some research when you go back to your hostel. Look at the number of words and vocabulary the books in the market have. Study the competition."

"We can tie up with schools for recommendation of our app," Chung added.

"Yes, play zones and nurseries too. You can have the app centrally installed in nurseries to story-tell children to bed. We can have audio books in the app," Keshav suggested, his mind opening up. "It can reduce the requirement of staff in the nurseries. That is a huge value proposition in fact. Please note it down, we will capture it in the unit economics."

"So, will there be a separate version for business to business and for business to customer?" Chung asked.

"Absolutely yes!" Keshav replied, elaborating on it further. "We will prepare financial models accordingly for both the segments. And price both based on their respective value propositions."

He then explained the business model canvas – the components of a business model.

Chung took notes.

She faired them when she was back in the hostel.

Jia spent hours researching children's books. She picked up books from stores to look at the way illustrations were done, improving her work day after day. She analyzed the books – the word count, the intent, type of words, and pictures used for various age groups.

Later in the evening, they worked together to align the product with the target markets.

"Here, these are the ones for the young lots, age two onward." Jia showed the stories to Chung.

"Perfect! So we can market those in the nurseries and pre-schools," Chung added.

"And these would be for older children," Jia said, giving her the other lot of stories.

"These would be marketed through schools, activity classes, and game centers," Chung replied. "Here, I've even prepared basic policy frameworks and workflows."

"These looks perfect, Chung!" Jia said, reading the workflows.

A wedge of sunlight pierced their hostel room window. The sky was losing its colors.

"The skyline looks amazing …" Jia said.

"Weather is great today too. Do you want to take a walk outside?" Chung asked.

Jia nodded.

They put aside their start-up and went down to walk along the sidewalk. The crescent moon rested over their heads.

"Chung, what is your favorite childhood memory?" Jia asked Chung.

"Walking in the park with māma and bàba when the cherry blossoms were in bloom … during summer. We went for picnic with our cousins and played chinese games together … Our childhood flew by … How about yours?"

Jia gulped. "My Sundays with my mother. We would head to the beach in the morning, play with the frisbee, and then draw on the beach sand. We'd eat chaat – Indian street food; Mumbai serves the best dabeli and vadapav …"

"Umm, what are these?" Chung asked.

"Fried potato, green chilli, garlic paste, and bun … they burst with flavour!" Jia expressed, "Wait, let me show you the images on Google …" She swiped through chaat pictures. "In fact, I'll take you for *panipuri* one of these days!" Jia was excited. "So by evening, Mummy and I would be tired. She would sing to me for a few minutes and I would sleep easily, with my head on her lap … In my dreams, I can still hear the melody …"

"Do you remember the song?" Chung asked.

Jia nodded and whispered the lyrics without the tune,

"Catch a falling star and put it in your pocket,

Save it for a rainy day…"

Chung put her arm through Jia's. "Do you want to listen to it together?"

"Right now?" Jia asked.

Chung nodded. "Mm-hmm!"

Jia put on the song and shared her earphones with Chung.

***

In the fifth and sixth sessions, Keshav Sir explained unit economics.

"Everything boils down to the viability of a start-up. Investments are made on financial predictions. We need investment to grow this – to develop the application and to acquire customers. Finance is the fuel that will help us rocket the start-up!"

He continued, "The biggest issue entrepreneurs are facing is their lack of financial answerability. They love their product – like you do. But none of them feel answerable toward the finances. They are driving the business without concern toward the profitability. Profitability is what will sustain the business. You can burn money for a year or two, but after that the company has to survive!"

"Eventually it is money which is important, isn't it?" Jia asked flatly. Her work was being reduced to something commercial! *What about my mother's footprint? Is that not important?* she thought.

"Yes, money is important. But let us understand why it is important, the right reasons. If a business is not profitable, it is a hobby. If it is a hobby, it comes with an expense. If you want to continue doing this, it must be profitable, else it will not sustain."

Jia did not look convinced. Keshav explained to her in a parental manner.

"Once you have your money matters solved, your stomach is full, your necessities are met, you can concentrate on things that matter more. Like love, charities, travel, meditation, or even food – whatever it is that you enjoy the most. You need to be secure and stable, taking care of your survival, yourself, correct? The same for a business. You will need to take care of your employees, correct? They have families back at home."

Jia fiddled with her pen, absorbing each word Keshav put out. She looked at him sheepishly.

"I understand your emotions, Jia. But the ways of the world have developed over time after deliberation. Don't overthrow them without giving them a chance. Currency is how value is exchanged."

No one had explained things to her, especially these practical things. No one had sat her down like a child and spoken about basic life things.

Maybe this is what having a father feels like, she thought.

She pondered over what Keshav had said. Everything made sense. It was exactly what Smriti had done – provided for Jia.

Life was fleeting with discussions of Mumsaga. It left Jia with little time to day dream. She became passionate about Mumsaga and opened up to the idea of being an entrepreneur. She thought about how she would want to spend her life, what she'd want to grow up to be. Though the answers to such questions led to "being like Keshav Sir", the caterpillar wanted wings.

The next month, she surprised herself by her artwork. Her hands sketched still art, painted sceneries, and sculpted with an opinion of their own, from a place of enhanced intuition. She extended her visions into manifestation, placing them on the canvas effectively.

"What have you sketched today, Jia?" her teacher asked in one of the classes.

"I've sketched a sustainable civilization that works on barter. The more organic the produce, the higher value it attracts for exchange. Same for clothing," Jia replied.

"That's novel. Why a marketplace?" the teacher asked.

"I was thinking about how value is exchanged," Jia replied.

Her classmates gathered around her to see her sketch. She interacted with them and made friends. Her peers were astounded with her imagination and credited the petite lass's surprising creativity.

During their eighth session with Keshav Sir, they discussed team building.

"You should have three founders: a business head, like Chung, a product head, like Jia, and a finance head. When we look for an investor, we will also look for someone to fill in that gap. Till then, both of you will work on the finances together. All founders should have knowledge of finance."

"My father says that too. Everyone should have financial knowledge. He was an accountant. He would say that while the marketing brings in the funds, finance is what saves and grows it!" Chung said.

Keshav said, "Coincidentally, my father was also an accountant. I learned it from him too."

At the mention of fathers, Jia's smile muted. *No father here,* she thought.

Keshav noticed and tried cheering her up. "You are one of the most talented artists I've met. I've worked with enough founders to recognize talent. You know how to layer your art, which is rare," Keshav praised her. Jia did not respond. He continued, *"Apne aap se pyaar karo, zindagi se pyaar karo.* (Love yourself, love life.)"

"How can one do that if they don't bear love for anything?" Jia asked him.

"By forgiving those who have wronged you, even forgiving life for being the way it is," Keshav replied. "Forgiveness will create space for love."

Happiness needs space to grow, Jia recalled Smriti's words.

***

"I had a tiring day. These extra credit classes are taking a toll on me," Chung said, dumping her college bag on her bed.

Jia was making a pinch-and-coil pot. Her apron was snug around her waist; it was the same length as her shorts.

"Clay is smudged all over your legs, Jia," Chung said. In the attempt to wipe it off, Jia spread the clay further.

She chuckled; her eyes lit up.

Chung looked around their room. There was a pile of Mumsaga artwork, a pile of Jia's school artwork, a sketch of her grandmother, tiny sculptures placed on their windowsill, along with her mother's Merlion.

"I never thought I'd be living with an artist …"

"Come, make this with me?" Jia offered.

"I can't get my hands dirty. I do like the smell in the room though, so earthy." Chung got up from her bed and sat next to Jia. "Do more of pottery … it's like room freshener."

"Try it, roll clay into a thick cord and place it on the pot maintaining the shape," Jia guided.

Chung poked the clay with her finger. "No, no, you make it, I'll watch."

Jia placed another coil, merging it with slip. Jia hummed.

"I have never seen you like this, Jia," Chung remarked.

"I'm enjoying our start-up," Jia replied. After a pause, she added, "I am also growing fond of Keshav Sir." Her eyes shimmered. "Chung, I used to wonder what my father was like. Whenever the thought strikes now, I imagine him to be someone like Keshav Sir."

"Aww. That is so sweet, Jia. You will miss him when the mentoring sessions end …"

"I hadn't thought of that. Would we have to stop interacting after that? How many sessions are left?" Jia asked.

"It will end with our semester. In three months," Chung replied.

Only three more months, she thought, and pinched the clay thinner.

CHAPTER TEN

Plant fleeting moments of joy,
And sprouts
A magical soul

KESHAV'S CHEST SWELLED with pride. "Girls, we have reached a milestone here today. You both are investment ready – I am not talking about your product or Mumsaga. But I am talking about the two of you. You have learned, worked hard, and adapted very well. Now whether you work in Mumsaga or any other start-up, you will shine as entrepreneurs. I am proud of how you have grown."

Another batch of student-preneurs, Keshav thought, his face beaming with self-fulfillment. This was his legacy – the number of entrepreneurs that leveraged onto his knowledge and wisdom.

"Thank you, Sir, my mother is exhilarated that you have mentored us. My resume will stand out with your name in it. I will get –" Chung began saying.

"Your resume will keep standing out if you keep standing out, Chung," Keshav said.

I can't believe I've become an entrepreneur now, Jia reflected. *It's only thanks to him.*

"A few more sessions and then we will meet for the investor pitch," Keshav announced.

Jia went back to her room, solemn. She crashed the moment she hit the bed.

Jia was sketching in her room, her music playing loudly. Booh, her soft toy lay on her bed. Smriti was calling her out for dinner.

"Lunch is ready," Smriti's voice could be heard above her hard rock.

Jia pushed open her bedroom door and walked toward the dining table. The dining table was a square shaped wooden one, and it had four chairs of different styles. The house was different, not her Mumbai apartment. Beams of sunlight lit the furnishings.

Sitting at the dining table were Smriti and Keshav Sir. Jia went and joined them.

"Why do you have to keep your room door closed all the time?" Smriti asked her.

"She needs her space, let her be," Keshav replied, handing her a casserole of paranthas.

Jia stared at them.

And woke up.

I'm dreaming about him too, Jia thought and pulled the quilt over her face. She put on music on her earphones and fell asleep.

Keshav noticed the melancholy in Jia's eyes waning. She had begun to laugh and sometimes cracked a joke or two herself. The stagnation had reduced, just like it had reduced for Smriti. His ability to make those two kids smile, especially Jia, had begun to fulfil him. After every session, Keshav went back home, a happier man, as if he had purpose in his life again.

In one of their last mentoring sessions together, Keshav said, "God bless you both. You are such sweet children, and your start-up is excellent. I am sure you will do wonders."

"Why God? What will he do?" Jia replied bluntly.

"He will watch over us!" Chung replied. Jia no longer surprised her.

"No, he will not. There is no such thing as God," Jia said, rolling her eyes.

"When we go through difficult times, we tend to believe the worst, don't we?" Keshav asked.

Jia frowned. "Those who don't know bad times are the ones that believe in God."

"In Sikhism we have this saying, '*Nanak, dukhiya sab sansar* – everyone has their share of sorrows'," Keshav said.

"Not everyone has equal pain," she said irritably. She did not want to show her role model her angry side.

"The timing of the problems, the intensity of the problems, the manifestation of it, may be different for different people. But everyone does have their karmas playing out for themselves. As for God, it is a matter of belief. If you believe that God exists, then God exists. If you believe he doesn't, then for you he doesn't," Keshav explained to Jia.

Jia did not look interested in the conversation.

Keshav continued, "I will quote Niels Bohr: 'In every human, there is a sense that something infinite has been lost.' To fill this loss, we either do infinite things – we seek human love, we seek passion, we make money, we build whatever others tell us is valuable, or what we believe is valuable, or we believe that the infinity that will complete us is in the universe, and is completing us already. We believe that this lost infinity is approachable, is right here in our heart or in the temple. We give this infinity a face, a name, a story. When we embrace Him, we feel whole. We no longer need to seek others things to complete us. It could be true; maybe there is no God, but there is faith. The concept of God is simply the concept of faith. You do not need to go by what I am saying; you can remember this for a time in life when you want to revisit your beliefs," Keshav continued.

"My mother believed in all this, and I saw her drown. There was no God or universe or infinity there to save her." Jia got angry and left the room.

She saw her mother drown? What could be more painful? Keshav's heart sank. *I shouldn't have unsettled her.*

Jia went to the restroom. She splashed water on her face. She looked at herself in the mirror. And splashed water again.

No God, she told herself. *There is no God!*

Chung came in from the back and hugged her from behind.

Jia turned back and observed her clear skin and blunt nose. Her anger eased.

"Jia … are you okay?" Chung asked, taking Jia's fingers in hers. Chung was three inches shorter than her.

Chung's brow furrowed.

Sweet, Jia thought. "Thank you for having my back," Jia murmured. She grazed Chung's cheek with her thumb before pressing a kiss there.

"I got you, Jia." Chung smiled gently. "Always."

Chung held Jia's hand tightly, her grip steady and reassuring, and led Jia back to the session.

"Come, we will not like God today. Don't worry," Keshav joked.

"Yeah, probably never," Jia whispered.

Chung and Keshav exchanged looks and giggled.

Watching the two of them, Jia smiled. The demons within her shrunk around these two.

"One can be virtuous without believing in this voodoo-divine thing. My mother and I did charities on our birthdays. Those children's smiles were enough; I did not need supernatural beliefs."

"Oh, is that so? A friend of mine also did that with her daughter on birthdays." Keshav recalled how amazing Smriti was with children.

Then it suddenly struck him. Smriti's daughter would be about the same age as Jia – she was around fourteen or fifteen when they had met almost four years ago now.

Another uncanny coincidence sunk in – *Smriti's daughter was agnostic.*

Keshav peered at Jia. Her hair was curly. Her eyes were hazel. Her nose was sharp.

He strained his mind to recall the pictures he had seen on the living room wall. But it had been years now, and it was a quick look. Didn't her daughter have curly hair and hazel eyes? Where was his brilliant memory when he needed it?

"What did you say your full name was?" Keshav's jittery, unsettled heart probed.

"Jia Jain," Jia spoke clearly.

A shiver ran through his spine.

Keshav's head was muddled – Mumbai, Jain, about the same age as Smriti's daughter, also agnostic. He gulped.

The universe of these things combined will be big, Keshav thought. *Non-conclusive that she has anything to do with Smriti.*

And Jia is an orphan. Smriti's daughter … well, has Smriti.

Chung shook Keshav out of his daze. "Sir, where are you lost? Is our session done?"

"I'm sorry, yes, we will wind up now."

***

"Girls, I am ready with my feedback for the professors. From my side, you are ready for launch. You could wait to kickstart your start-up after the second year of college is over so you can give your exams fairly. Because once you start it, there will be work on your hands. The college will exempt you from some classes and give you credits, but it is better to finish off the ongoing year. All the best, girls. I will be at the investor meet. I am proud of both of you."

"Why can't you invest in it if you are proud and confident?" Jia asked.

"Fair question. A third person investor would be a better validation of your business than someone who has been involved for six long months. You will take me and my involvement lightly, lah! Let the sharks drive you to do better!"

Jia sighed. *Is there no way that he can be around longer?*

Keshav took a demo presentation from them, grilling them over the pointers that the investor might ask of them.

He asked Chung how long she intended to work with Mumsaga. Chung got stuck at the question.

"I will continue even if Chung does not," Jia replied.

"Then you will need another business head," Keshav said.

Jia nodded.

They had completed six months together. This beautiful dream of a relationship was going to end along with the mentorship program. Their sessions were filling up hollows of joy and trust in Jia's chest. She was alive, but Keshav Sir would go his way and she would be left alone once again.

Finally, the day arrived when Mumsaga would be pitched to investors. The main seats of the auditorium were occupied by representatives of venture capitalists. Entrepreneurship students were sitting in pockets, taking down notes from the pitches. Two start-ups out of five had already pitched their idea, and Mumsaga was up next.

Chung and Jia stood backstage, pacing the green room, revising their presentation.

"Chung, check if Keshav Sir has joined in the crowd yet," Jia asked.

"I can't see him, Jia," Chung replied.

"He promised us he'd be there," Jia grumbled. "Doesn't he care?"

She paced around the room, nervous.

"Do you think they will like it? Will they validate the product?" Jia asked Chung.

"Of course, they would!" Keshav's sweet voice reached out in response. Jia turned around and saw that he was standing behind them in the green room. He was wearing a blue suit, and a white shirt; the shirt fabric snug tighter around his belly.

"You're here," Jia murmured, her hazel eyes twinkling.

"Of course, I wouldn't miss your investor pitch!" Keshav said. "I'm sorry I'm late though, how were the first two? The sharks would only want to invest in one or maximum two of the companies, so you are up against the rest of them."

"Ah, competition!" Chung pronounced.

"Now go on, they are waiting for you!" Keshav nudged them. "Listen, mind the one sitting in the center in the pink checkered shirt. He will grill you the most, but don't get nervous. You are well prepared. Chung explains the business model; Jia creates a story to close the presentation."

"Story?" Jia asked. "Last minute you want me to come up with a story, Sir?"

"You do not need to come up with it, it is within you. Talk about why you want to do this and your journey. You have come a long way, Jia." Keshav smiled gently, his eyes shining.

"I cannot talk about my life, my journey. I have never done that," Jia said.

It was a déjà vu moment for Keshav. He had nudged Smriti into telling her story in the support group meeting too.

"Try it, as much as you are comfortable with. Speak one sentence at a time, and let it flow out naturally," Keshav advised Jia in the exact same words he had said to Smriti, years back.

"I can't speak in public about my life," Jia said.

"Talk to them as if you're talking to me," Keshav said, meeting her eyes. The hazel eyes didn't let go of the gaze.

He is the first person in five years who I want to trust, Jia thought, and a swarm of butterflies rose to her chest. Smriti's words rang in her ears. *You will trust people again, I promise.*

But he will go away after this, Mummy, Jia spoke back to Smriti in her mind.

This girl reminds me of Smriti. Smriti's daughter would be older now, she might want to give it another shot, Keshav thought. *Shall I call Smriti after this?*

Keshav and Jia stood facing each other, thinking of Smriti.

Chung snapped her fingers and brought them back to where they were.

"HELLO! We have to present now!" she cried shrilly. She turned to Jia. "Concentrate on this, you've worked hard."

Jia nodded.

"All the best, girls," Keshav said and left them to sit in the auditorium.

Chung held Jia's hand and took her to the stage.

As Chung finished explaining the business model with vigor, Jia took on the closing speech. She had never spoken in public before. She had never shared anything about her life before.

Where should she start?

She froze. Keshav was sitting in the audience; his face was glowing. His eyes met hers; he nodded and mouthed, "Go on."

Jia nodded.

"I was a single-parent child. I lost that parent three years back. Saying that I was shattered would be understating it. I was living in the shadows, despising things around me. I built illusions and lived in a parallel reality. I think the correct term for it is, maladaptive daydreaming. When I came to Singapore, though I did not intend to, I met this amazing friend, Chung. One day, she needed a start-up idea and I offered her my mother's stories and my sketches to assist her. But then I heard Keshav Sir speak of legacy and footprints. What Chung and I held in our hands was my mother's legacy. With the weight of it, I worked hard. I wanted to make my mother shine through this start-up. What I did not realize, though, is that while I wanted her to shine, I was healing. My mother was taking care of me through her stories. From darkness, I gradually shifted into light. Mumsaga is not only my mother's legacy, it is my torch." Jia paused, looking at how gravely the investors were listening to her before she continued.

"Today, I stand before you, able to envision a future for myself and this company. Mumsaga will always be lit by the same light that enlivened me. I will fight for its success. I will stand by Mumsaga like it stood for me. For that reason, I request you to invest in us."

Everyone in the meeting hall was stunned by Jia's speech. There was not a single dry eye. Keshav was also dabbing his eyes.

The saga was sold, and Mumsaga got the investment amount they needed. The start-up was incubated. All the professors, students, and student-preneurs gathered around the girls to congratulate them.

Jia chatted with one person after another, but her heart was scouting for Keshav Sir. She shuffled away from the crowd to go meet him.

Where is he? Jia thought, desperately looking around. *Has he gone already?*

She ran outside the auditorium and saw the familiar middle-aged man.

She stopped at a distance from him. *How? How could I ask a middle-aged man to continue being a part of my life? How could I ask him to inspire me and explain life to me? How could he be family?*

"Keshav Sir!" Jia approached him.

"Congratulations," Keshav said with a smile.

What could make him stay?

"Hey Jia, what is wrong?" Keshav asked.

"It is nothing, Sir," Jia responded flatly, her heart crashing.

"Are you missing your mother?" Keshav asked in a soft, calming voice.

Jia's eyes brimmed. She couldn't speak anything.

Keshav wanted to hug her, like he would have hugged Lily. By making Jia smile, he wanted to save Lily, he wanted to keep Kaveer happy, he wanted to make Smriti laugh.

Smriti, why can't I stop thinking about her, he thought. *I will call her at night.*

Jia gazed at him. And he gazed at her.

Chung joined them. "THANK YOU, SIR," she said and bowed. "And thank you, Jia. My parents here are saying thank you too." She was chatting with her mother in Chinese on video call.

"Good luck to you girls now." He smiled and nodded. "Go roam about Sentosa Island or the Universal Studios while you can. You have work to do after that, college lectures and a start-up! Oh, and you may see the Merlion, if you haven't till now. It is magnificent."

Jia's insides leaped at the mention of the Merlion. Keshav walked away, leaving the girls to themselves.

"Do you want to go see the Merlion with me?" Jia asked Chung.

"I will go back to the room; I have a college presentation next week that I should work on. But you should carry on. Celebrate, Jia. Big milestone," Chung replied.

Keshav was also thinking of Smriti. So, he headed to see the Merlion in her memory.

He drove from the auditorium to the Merlion Park. The breeze from the Singapore River was cool, but the sun shone brightly. The modern skyline cut through the colors of the sunset.

The cement statue stood tall. Two animals, a lion and a fish, were merged into one. The statue spouted a jet of water from the lion's mouth, and the promenade pulsated with the whistle of the fountain.

Keshav walked around the Merlion, thinking about his conversation with Smriti. "*I think about you. If you can give it another shot …*"

As he walked along the promenade, he snapped his fingers and began to hum *"Likhe jo khat tujhe … Jo teri yaad mein … Hazaaro rang ke, nazaare bann gaye …"*

"Sir, please don't sing that song," Jia's voice took him by surprise. "It makes me uncomfortable."

He turned around. Amidst the buzzing tourists clicking pictures, Jia stood in her formal clothes. Her curly hair was frizzy with the humidity.

"Hey, what are you doing here? Chung didn't come along?" he asked, smiling. He was holding his blazer in his arm. His shirt was tucked out.

"Chung wanted to finish her presentation. You suggested that we see the city. I stopped here since it reminded me of my mother. What are you doing here?" Jia explained, excited to see him outside of college. They had only met in their meeting room.

"It reminded me of someone too," he said, glancing at the Merlion. "Why don't you like Rafi? How can Rafi make anyone uncomfortable? Why would anyone dislike Indian music?"

Jia contemplated whether or not to open up about it. Then the words slipped through her mouth, "My mother used to listen to it …" Jia submitted, her eyes darting from her shoes to meet his eyes again.

An icy cold emotion trickled through his warm insides, pricking him harshly. Mumbai, Jain, similar age, those curls, and that hint on her face, Merlion reminded her of her mother, Rafi reminded her of her mother, and she was agnostic!

He was no longer disillusioned.

He straightened his spine.

His eyes leaked desperation.

"I'm sorry. But your mother, you say, used to listen to Rafi?" Keshav met the deep hazel eyes.

With the stillest mind, the heaviest heart, and yet the most hopeful vibration he prayed, *please God, please do not let Jia be Smriti's child.*

"Sorry Sir, but why are you upset that my mother used to listen to Rafi?" Jia asked, raising her voice to counter the expression on Keshav's face.

"Smriti?! Was your mother Smriti?" Keshav fumbled, afraid of the answer.

Jia nodded, stunned. *How did Keshav Sir know Mumma?*

His cheeks glistened with tears. He dug his face in his hands.

"Please, I beg of you, please tell me you've had a fight with her and she's back at home, healthy and thriving!" His throat constricted, and his breathing was rapid.

Jia shook her head hastily. A tear rolled down her cheek.

"No … no more."

Keshav turned around and let out a cry. He shook his head and covered his eyes with his hands. With his back to the confused teenager, he cried.

Smriti had passed away.

I was not there for her. I can't believe my ears, I can't believe life, I can't believe God, he thought, crying.

Jia stepped toward him, puzzled.

"Sir, why are you crying?" Jia asked, wiping the tears that pricked her cheeks. Then she knew it. "My mother had mentioned she met someone in her dreams. It was right before she passed away. Were you that person?"

Keshav turned around to face her. He pulled her into a comforting hug.

"Yes, I am. I loved her. I am so sorry, I'm so sorry, my child," he consoled the extremely confused Jia along with himself. "I'm so sorry." He sobbed.

Watching him cry, Jia's tears ran free too. It opened the dungeon which held the harshest memory, and unleashed the agony she had boxed up.

She dug her face into his warm chest and wrapped her arms around his squishy belly as she wept and screamed.

"She left me alone!" Jia yelled through her tears, her body shaking with the despair that lay buried.

Keshav dried his tears to care for Jia.

"She left both of us. You are not alone. I am here for you," Keshav replied, overwhelmed, betrayed by fate.

"I am here for you," he said again. "How, Jia? How did something like this even happen? Was she unwell?" Keshav asked Jia with a heavy heart, wondering if she had been unwell when they'd met, wondering if that was the reason she had let go of him. And then he remembered, drowning. Smriti had drowned.

"Mumbai floods. She went down a manhole," Jia muttered with quivering lips. Her body refused to let go of the pain. Yet her soul, in the arms of a soulmate, in the arms of a father it craved, relinquished.

"They found her body the next day … my Mumma …"

Keshav's heart was severed.

Mumbai flood! A manhole took the mightiest of women away!

"I'm so sorry."

"This is unbelievable," Jia whispered. Keshav Sir, someone she admired deeply, was her late mother's love.

Jia looked at him. His soft, loving eyes were filled with sorrow.

Over an hour ago she thought she was going to lose this person, that this relationship was about to come to an end because the mentorship program was ending. And here she was, standing before him, forging a relationship.

"Come, let's take a walk together," he said to her, running his hand over her hair.

Neither of them spoke. They were both reminiscing about their respective memories of Smriti. Keshav put his arm around her shoulder, and she leaned into him. They walked for ten minutes, listening to the multi-lingual chatter of tourists that surrounded them and the soft fall of the fountain. The dusky sky sheltered them as after a long time, the two of them experienced "home" together.

"Can I take you for dinner tomorrow night? We have a lot to talk about," Keshav asked.

"Yes." Jia nodded.

She could not believe how the last twenty minutes had been spent.

***

Keshav went back to his house in the evening and poured himself a glass of whiskey.

Jia is Smriti's daughter. Smriti is no more.

He poured a second glass of whiskey. His heart needed support.

Should I have fought harder for her? Why did I let her go without a fight? Now, I'll never get that chance …

He poured a third glass for himself. As the smoky flavors of the whiskey filled his grieving insides, he took out his phone and Googled Smriti Jain, looking for articles from three years back. He found it.

"Two died after falling into open manhole, heavy rain lashes Mumbai."

Keshav scrolled through the article. It spoke of the carelessness of the officials, the dire need to act, and the situation remaining unresolved even after many such deaths. Keshav minimized the screen with a solemn heart.

It was an unfair way to have died. With a young daughter, an incomplete life.

He twirled the whiskey glass in his hand. He cried and then controlled it. *Jia* ... The baby pictures came back to him. Those curls, those chubby rosy cheeks, those cute hazel eyes.

How has Jia landed right in front of me? What kind of tricks has the universe been playing with us?

He thought about their time together – Smriti's forgiving smile when Mahesh had taken her parking slot; the trek they had been on; the songs they had sung in the bus; her fingers intertwined in his; the glances he had taken when she was looking at the sea …

He went out to the balcony of his penthouse.

Smriti, where'd you go? Can you hear my thoughts?

Are you hiding behind a cloud, Remembrance?

Tears rolled down his cheeks.

You're with my daughter and I'm with yours. Jia's not alone anymore, Smriti … I'll take care of her … I'll take care of her.

***

Jia borrowed a black halter dress from Chung. She looked at herself in the mirror.

"I'm getting ready after three years. Last, I had gotten ready was for my dinner with Mumma during our holiday together …" Jia told Chung.

I look so different, from sixteen to nineteen, my acne has gone, Jia thought, tracing her forehead with her fingers.

"Wear a lip balm," Chung said, handing her one. "Just a transparent one."

Jia turned around and saw Chung. She quietly took the lip balm and applied it on her lips. Her grace enhanced her eccentricity.

"I still can't believe Keshav Sir knew your mother," Chung said, shaking her head.

"Yeah, me neither …" Jia replied, savoring how good she felt about it. Her heart had accepted him easily.

At sharp 6 p.m., Keshav picked Jia up for dinner.

Jia sat in his car beside him.

"Hi," Keshav replied, extending his hand.

"Hi," Jia replied, smiling and taking his hand.

"All good?" Keshav asked.

"Yeah, all good." Jia nodded.

Jia increased the volume of the stereo. She squinted her eyes before rolling them. *I can see what an easy pair they might have been.*

"Do you want to listen to my music for a change? It will be real fun after these depressing old Hindi things that you and mom tripped on," Jia suggested.

"Sure, what kind of music do you listen to?" Keshav grinned.

"I also listen to old songs, but teeny-bit different from the old songs you listen to." Jia played "Stairway to Heaven".

"Okay, okay." Keshav smiled as he heard the song.

"Now, tell me, how did you and Mumma meet?"

"We met in a support group in Mumbai, about four years back now," Keshav said, his heart solemn.

"I know of that group. It was right before the time…" She left out the words, *I attempted suicide.*

"Before what time?" Keshav asked.

Jia contemplated and decided to keep it for later.

"Before I came back home from boarding school," Jia said.

"Yes, Smriti was about to speak with you about us, but when she brought you back, she cut contact with me," Keshav told her.

I'm sorry you guys lost contact because of me, she thought.

"I don't understand why she cut contact. You wouldn't have minded if we were together right?" Keshav murmured.

Jia gazed out at the moving traffic. "How did you not recognize me?"

"I didn't know your name, and I hadn't seen any grown picture of you. When I saw you, I was reminded of Smriti, but I thought it was my mind playing tricks," Keshav admitted. "You have her nose. Your hair is different, and your eye color."

"Yes," Jia said.

Keshav drove to the restaurant, pondering over his last conversation with Smriti. She had skipped calls while she was in Indore … She had said that she needed to be there for her daughter and was distracted from her duties.

They reached the restaurant, and took a table for two. Both Jia and Keshav were mulling over their thoughts. The attendant disturbed the comfortable silence between the two.

"Okay, vegetarian, right?"

"Jia Jain." Jia nodded.

He ordered a four-course meal. "I eat when I am stressed. How about you? Do you binge eat when you are stressed?"

"Sir, look at me. Do you think I relish food?" Jia chuckled. "The first meal I enjoyed after mom, was when I reached Singapore."

"I've still not absorbed … Where did you stay after?" Keshav asked.

"I moved in with mum's friends, Lata Aunty and Mohit Uncle. They were excellent hosts. They helped me through. I talk to Avantika often, their daughter."

"Oh yes, I remember she had one friend in Mumbai," Keshav recalled.

"You have a wife and a son?" Jia asked.

"Yes, ex-wife, they are in Kerala. He comes during break. On Diwali, I will see him."

Food arrived amidst their talks, and a hungry Keshav dived right in.

"Did you know the Chinese add superstitious symbols to their food? They have dumplings of different shapes to increase wealth and improve health, etcetera?" Keshav changed the topic randomly.

"No, I didn't know." Jia smiled.

"Can you teach me how to use the chopsticks?" Jia asked Keshav, struggling to use them and embarrassed to ask for a fork.

"Place the first one at the web of your thumb… this stays still. And the other, you hold like a pen, this one moves. Like this, see …" Keshav illustrated and taught Jia.

Looking at Keshav eat and wondering what the fuss was about, Jia dug into the meal.

This is amazing! she thought. She hogged quietly.

"Sir, I've overeaten!"

"With me around, you will gain some kilos. Actually, I was wondering, would you like to have dinner with me every Wednesday?" Keshav took a leap of faith.

"Yes, I would love that." Jia smiled.

She was upset about losing Keshav when he was a mentor, and now he was more. They had a connection, a personal bond that, though difficult to explain by societal norms yet, was surreal in their world. They both had lost Smriti, were alone and incomplete in their lives; they both craved family.

Keshav's eyes twinkled.

"Your salt has taken over the pepper in the last six months," Jia remarked.

"How does it look? Do you think I need to dye my hair?" Keshav asked genuinely. "I should just shave off and get rid of all of it."

Jia giggled. "No, no!"

Keshav drove Jia back.

She turned around and smiled to say goodbye.

"I'm glad you were a part of my mother's life."

CHAPTER ELEVEN

The light bestowed during darkness
Is the truest manifestation of God's love
Clutch this little something called family,
the chosen family

KESHAV PICKED JIA up for their Wednesday dinner.

"Hi," Keshav said.

"Hi, I remember this T-shirt; you'd worn it at the mentor meet!" Jia replied.

"Ahh, does fashion interest you?"

"You think? I borrow clothes from Chung. That black dress was hers; this red top is hers," Jia said, tugging at the ruffles on her neck. The two pairs of jeans she brought from India had lasted her two years. She enjoyed styling her hair though. She had tucked her curls with a pin.

"Where can I shop here?" Jia asked.

"There are a few malls. I can take you sometime," Keshav offered.

"Okay, I will ask Chung to tag along. It will reduce my botheration," Jia replied.

"What are you planning for Mumsaga now? Did you have an investor meeting?"

"Yes, we did. They suggested Chung should be on board for the initial one year, after that we can have someone else."

"Did they offer any leverage? What can they assist with?" Keshav asked.

"Building the tech," Jia replied.

"Hmm." Keshav nodded.

They parked the car and went into the restaurant.

"Kimchi, pickled cabbage." Keshav dug his chopsticks into the kimchi bowl while waiting for the appetizers.

"Doesn't sound appetizing!"

"No, it is amazing … here, try!" Keshav picked up another chunk of kimchi and placed it on Jia's plate.

Jia winced as she placed a piece in her mouth. "Spicy, tangy, nice." She nodded and took another bite.

Their starters came and they relished their stir-fried edamame and dim sums.

"I was five when I noticed that a set of two parents came for the annual day. I was the only one in my class without a father. When I asked mom where mine was, she told me she was my two parents. I know she loved me, but I never found that answer enough. What about my dad? Where is he? Why is he not around, you know? Why am I the unlucky one with one parent? For years, I questioned where my father was. And then I got immune to my quest. When I was about nine, one of my friends' parents asked what my father did for a living. They did not know that I did not have one. I lied in response. I told them he was in the navy. After that, whenever people asked me about him, I made stuff up …"

The moment Jia shared her feelings with Keshav, a beam of light from the universe healed her dark dungeon. The inner quest, discomfort, and turmoil regarding her father subdued.

Keshav replied, "With time one understands that it is the quality of family that matters, not the number. I can second that your mother loved you enough for two people. She was fretful the day she could not call you from the trek. She asked everyone for their phones, trying your school's number all day."

Jia flushed, ashamed that she had taken the disastrous step at the time. *Shall I tell him? Maybe later on …*

"Did I tell you I had a daughter whom I lost when she was two?" Keshav shared.

Jia shook her head. "I am sorry that you lost her," she said, reaching over the table and placing her palm over his.

"I planned my second child thinking we would be the ideal family. But in a few years, I went from a family of four to being alone. After it fell apart, I longed for a single person to genuinely form my home," Keshav admitted.

"We had that in the same person, didn't we?" Jia asked him.

"Yes, I found that home in Smriti. We were together for a short while, but I could envision a happy life with her," Keshav replied, fiddling with his chopsticks.

After a moment's silence, Keshav spoke again.

"Why don't you come by for lunch on Sunday?" Keshav asked.

"Do you cook?" Jia asked, surprised.

"I do. I might not be as good as Smriti, but I can try my hand at the rajma chawal you used to love. It is a Punjabi dish after all!" Keshav smiled, putting his wit to great use.

"Sunday lunch it is, Sir!" Jia smiled.

"Okay, and this 'Sir' thing needs to stop. I was hoping I was more than a mentor by now," Keshav slipped in cheekily.

"You are way more than a mentor. But what would I call you then?" Jia asked.

"I don't know. Figure it out. Call me Keshav till then," Keshav stated.

***

She entered Keshav's penthouse at around noon on Sunday.

Keshav opened the door on the third bell.

"Sorry, I had my hands full." He grinned through his teeth, giving Jia a side hug. "Come on in, bacha."

Jia was carrying brownies for them to binge on after lunch.

Keshav was wearing an apron and smelled like desi ghee himself. The house smelled of the masala that he had browned for the rajma.

The door opened into a huge living room, which was furnished in a sleek modern fashion. The furniture was straight-line and the upholstery was balanced between gray and beige, with highlights of navy blue. Placed opposite the sofas was a big television. Instead of a wall on the left, there were massive windows that exhibited the high rises of the city. The apartment was flooded with sunlight.

Keshav had busied himself in the spacious modular open kitchen.

"Please make yourself comfortable," Keshav said loudly, gesturing toward the sofas from across the kitchen.

It had been a long while since she had watched television. She picked up the remote from the entertainment unit. As she was turning toward the sofas, her eyes fell on a photo-frame which had Keshav's son's picture, another frame with the four of them, and a small, Gateway of India made of clay.

Her heart swelled thinking of how he had preserved the Gateway of India, like Smriti had preserved the Merlion in her living room.

"Is that Kaveer?" Jia asked as confirmation.

"Yes. Good looking, no? Takes after his father?" Keshav joked around.

"I'm a nineteen-year-old girl who is uncomfortable about commenting on the looks of a fellow teenager," Jia replied, smiling.

Also, I don't find boys attractive, Jia thought, as she sprawled on the living room sofas.

Flipping through Netflix, she told Keshav that she had seen the Merlion in Smriti's living room.

"It was why I was there by the Merlion that day. It never made sense to me why she had it, until now," Jia said. "In fact, coincidentally, while I was flying from Mumbai, I had sketched a caricature of yours," Jia confessed sheepishly.

"What do you mean by that?" Keshav asked, intrigued by the idea of it. He took his attention away from the cooking range and turned to look at her as she replied.

"So, I saw your face on the cover of a magazine and decided to draw a caricature of it." Jia met Keshav's eyes as she told him. "Of course, I didn't know how we would connect later on."

"Your mother believed in destiny." Keshav smiled.

"Yeah, she did ..."

Jia's heart was fuzzy. She flipped through OTT. Ever since her Mumsaga pitch, she had an interest in start-ups. She put on a show that was created around start-ups and investments.

She watched Keshav from the corner of her eyes as he stirred the dishes he was cooking.

I'm going to love him, she thought, beaming with gratitude.

Where there were screaming dungeons of pain, now there was tenderness and affection. It was all because of this heaven-sent cuddly man, cooking lunch for her.

"I cannot believe that this girl I met nine months back, completely averse to business and finance, is watching *Shark Tank* today," Keshav announced in a sing-song manner, listening to the show from a distance, as he turned off the ignition of the dishes.

"All thanks to you," Jia almost said Sir, and then stopped.

Keshav came and sat on the adjoining sofa, taking off his apron.

They watched *Shark Tank* together, discussing who should and who should not get investment, whose story had promise, and then switched to discussing the prospects of Mumsaga.

They moved from the living room to the dining table, digging into their favorite meal together.

"Damn, this is yummy," Jia said, taking a bite of the hot rajma.

"As yummy as Smriti's?" Keshav asked.

"Actually, being entirely honest, if it is possible, this is better," Jia confessed with a bursting heart.

"See Smriti, I told you I cook better than you! You know, we teamed up to make sushi together and she was terrible at it!" Keshav said out loud, his heart pining for the love that was snatched away from him.

"Oh, I know of that sushi expedition! Mom and sushi is a bad combination! She was so simple." Jia smiled.

"She was … and so genuine and so sweet," Keshav said.

"We got her ear pierced, you know!" Jia recalled.

"Oh no, I loved her no-piercing look." Keshav smiled.

They basked in their love for Smriti.

"It is her birthday in September. Let us celebrate it together," Jia suggested.

"Yes, we can watch *Veer Zara* couched here," Keshav added.

"She loved that lame movie!"

Jia's fairy tale was complete. She had found her lost parent.

"Keshav, the reason why mom cut you off … the reason why she didn't tell me about you, was because I attempted suicide," Jia yielded in a low whisper.

"You attempted suicide in school?" Keshav asked.

Jia nodded.

"My God, what all has this child been through!" he said, pulling her into a hug. "But why? Because of the bullying?"

"How much did you two speak in two months!"

"Measured time doesn't matter in the larger scheme of things … Days, months, or years, the truth in the connection matters, that's all," Keshav said, "But beta, you should connect with a therapist."

Jia smiled and dug her face into his chest. He ruffled her hair. "What all are you holding within yourself?"

Jia winced, holding onto her final secret.

***

As September came, Jia and Keshav couched into their sofa sets. Keshav had ordered in donuts expecting himself to cry during *Veer Zara.*

"Look at your growing tummy, you'll get diabetes," Jia said with concern.

"Have you gained any weight in my company?" Keshav asked back, ignoring her comment.

"Three kilos in one year," Jia replied, sticking out her elbows and fluffing her mouth.

"I can still see your bones sticking out," Keshav said, passing her a donut. "Here, this one has chocolate cream; hand me the raspberry one."

They motioned "cheers" with their donuts.

"Happy birthday, Mummy," Jia said, biting into the donuts.

"Happy birthday, *Remembrance*," Keshav added.

When Veer Pratap Singh went to jail for Zara Hayaat Khan, Keshav turned his head away from the film and Jia because he was uncontrollable.

"So much you cry!" Jia muttered, splitting the last donut into two and handing him the other half. "It is a movie, relax now . . ." She hugged him. "I will have to pause it if you don't stop crying."

"No, no, we'll finish it," Keshav said in between sobs.

"Kaveer will be here for Diwali. Are you ready to officially be part of the family?" Keshav asked.

"How will he respond to me?" Jia asked.

"He has an accepting heart, but let's see. Don't worry. The three of us will spend Diwali together," Keshav said. "Bring Chung along!"

While Keshav asked Jia not to worry, he was sweaty himself. He ran the conversations in his head.

***

Keshav paced outside the airport, waiting for Kaveer's flight to land. He was nervous about how he'd introduce Jia to him.

Should I tell him that she was a student? Should I tell him about Smriti?

But when he saw him, he forgot all about the conversation.

"Hi Papa!" Kaveer hollered from the gate.

Keshav waved vigorously, and Kaveer came running toward him, giving him a bear hug.

"You're six feet now!" Keshav claimed. "Taller than your Papa!"

"I dropped out of college, Papa. Thanks to you, I am no longer doing engineering!" Kaveer beamed. "I'm free for a few months."

"How much time out of those months do I get?" Keshav asked.

"I'm thinking of staying here for all of it, before my college starts again," Kaveer said, ushering his luggage to the parking lot.

"Wow!" Keshav said excitedly. "What does Mom have to say about it?" Keshav asked, surprised that Neha had sent Kaveer for such a long time.

"She's so upset about my decision to study Humanities that staying with you is the lesser of her concerns," Kaveer said, grinning.

"Yeah, she did not expect it," Keshav said. "You're happy, right?"

"Of course I am! I have been interested in politics since school!" Kaveer said.

"You can also explore journalism then," Keshav suggested, sitting in the car. He drove Kaveer to their apartment.

"Singapore hasn't changed in the past ten years, has it?" Kaveer asked.

"Not much. Do you think of studying here?" Keshav asked.

"Maybe after graduation," Kaveer said.

Kaveer entered the apartment. He placed his luggage in his old room. Even after eight years, Keshav hadn't changed anything. His posters from school still filled the walls.

"Aaah, this room!" He crashed on his bed.

Coming out to the living room, he noticed the pictures Keshav had gotten framed.

Lily … He saw the picture of the four of them.

"Your house smells of Indian food, Papa," Kaveer said, scrunching his nose.

"Yes, we've trained didi to cook daal makhani," Keshav said without thinking.

"Who is 'we' here?" Kaveer said, scrutinizing the apartment.

Keshav buried his face in his palms.

"There is this girl, exactly your age …"

"Papa, please, you're disgusting me," Kaveer spoke, revolted. "I shouldn't have come here. I was better off with Mom."

He paced the living room.

"Yes but, you're presuming wrong," Keshav said frantically. He was sitting on his sofa. Kaveer hovered over him.

Teenage boys, Keshav thought.

"Please sit down and listen," Keshav tried. "She is my friend's daughter."

"What is a teenage girl doing at your place?" Kaveer was angry and confused.

"She's become like a daughter to me …" Keshav submitted.

"How?" Kaveer asked, frazzled. "How has someone become like a child to you?"

"Well, I mentored her and then got to know that her mother had passed away. I knew her mother closely. She has never had a father. She is an orphan."

"Huh," Kaveer said. "So, she hangs out with you?"

"Yeah, kind of. I take her for dinner on Wednesdays," Keshav said.

"But why?" Kaveer asked.

"Because she doesn't have family either," Keshav replied. "And to be honest, I get lonely. Neha took you with her. Nobody even thought about how I'd feel without my kids."

Kaveer sat on the sofa. "Do you get lonely?"

"Obviously I get lonely. I've eaten dinner alone for eight years. I long to spend time with you, and search for you in the kids I mentor. It's why I joined the university. I understand that it is an unusual dynamic, but Kaveer, I am lucky to have found family in this girl."

"I'm sorry I didn't know it gets lonely for you. What's her name?"

"Jia. Jia Jain. We will spend Diwali together. Is that okay?"

Kaveer nodded.

"So, I don't have a stepmother?" he asked.

Keshav shook his head, thinking, *I wish you did.*

***

Kaveer and Keshav had decorated the penthouse with candles and diyas. They both were wearing matching kurta and pajamas.

"You can think of modeling as a career too," Keshav suggested. "My Kerala-Punjabi boy."

Kaveer grinned. "We will keep it as my back-up option."

Didi had made daal makhani, coconut curry, and Malabar parantha.

The doorbell rang. He opened the door to two lean girls. A tall, curly-haired, hazel-eyed one wearing a salwar suit, and a medium-height Chinese girl wearing a kurta with jeans.

"Hi Kaveer," Jia said, extending her hand for Kaveer to shake. "Happy Diwali."

"Happy Diwali, Jia and?" Kaveer turned toward Chung.

"Chung," Chung said, giggling.

Kaveer led them inside to the candle-and-diya-lit dining area. Chung looked at Jia, and mouthed, "He is yummy!"

Jia shrugged.

"All my kids are here," Keshav hollered. "Happy Diwali, children."

"Happy Diwali." Jia side-hugged Keshav and seated herself at the dining table.

"Happy Diwali, Keshav Sir," Chung said, taking the seat next to Jia.

"Happy Diwali," Kaveer added. "Have you seen the Diwali celebrations at Singapore's Little India, Jia?"

Jia shook her head. "No, I haven't. Last year I was in the hostel room."

"Next year we can probably take her there, Papa," Kaveer told Keshav.

Jia and Keshav exchanged looks. "Thank you, Kaveer," Jia added.

Chung had already begun eating. "Wow, Indian food is delicious!" she said, stuffing her mouth with parantha and curry. "I've taken a few bites from Jia's meals at the mess, but those are terrible in comparison to this."

"That's terrible anyway," Jia said.

Kaveer looked at her. "We've called for rasmalai for dessert. Would you have preferred something else?"

"I haven't had Indian desserts in years now. Rasmalai is amazing. Though we shouldn't give Keshav any, he's prediabetic."

"Oh yes! He has gained more weight also," Kaveer added. "No rasmalai for Papa."

"Stop kids, don't do that to me!" Keshav whined.

"What is rasssmalayee?" Chung asked, between two hurried bites.

"The best Indian dessert there ever was!" Keshav added.

"What are you doing in college?" Jia asked Kaveer.

"I have dropped a year … planning on taking up political science. You?"

"Arts …" Jia replied.

As the kids finished their meals and pushed Keshav away from the dining table so he wouldn't get tempted by the desserts, Keshav went out to his terrace. He thought about the many festivals he'd spent alone. *Smriti, you sent me the children, didn't you?*

***

The following day, Keshav took the kids to the gurudwara and they lit candles together.

"Take us to the Jain mandir," Keshav said.

"I'm not religious," Jia replied flatly.

"For my sake," Keshav said, remembering his promise to Smriti to make her a questioner at least.

"Even I would love to go," Kaveer pressed.

"We are two against one. Sorry, you lose." Keshav shrugged.

Jia rolled her eyes.

With Keshav and Kaveer trailing behind her, Jia walked into the Jain temple after five years. Her heart beat fast. She showed them the rosary beads they could use for chanting. They sat in meditation for a while. Before she finished her 108 beads, she broke down.

I miss you, Mummy, Jia thought. *God, why did you separate us?*

As she addressed God, the supernatural touched her spirit. A warm sensation flooded her heart chakra. The frost melted.

"Is she is watching us from somewhere?" Jia asked Keshav.

Keshav smiled. The temple had achieved what Smriti would have wanted for Jia.

"Not only is she watching over us, but she has brought us together." Her tears fell, and in the presence of God, in the presence of her chosen family, Jia healed.

EPILOGUE

IT HAD BEEN six years for Mumsaga.

Avantika had taken up a course in Singapore. She had reduced binge-eating and was dropping sizes by the year. As planned, she and Jia toured around Singapore and Malaysia together.

Kaveer was working at a news channel, focusing on political news. He was preparing to be a journalist.

Chung had moved to Boston. Her parents lived with her, and she worked long hours as an investment banker. While Jia had found other partners at Mumsaga, Chung remained her best friend.

A web application was built for children of varied age groups, and every year they launched two new series of children's books. They had even given out rights for hard copy publishing of the books. Smriti's children's books were thriving in the retail stores.

Jia's mailbox buzzed with sponsorships and collaboration emails.

But Jia was bothered even amidst the busy hours at Mumsaga.

Her phone pinged with a text. It was Keshav.

"Pick you up at 6?"

There's never going to be a good time for this, I have to tell him now, Jia thought.

She took out the sketch she had drawn. Two closets – one closet with a caricature of Jia in it, the other closet with a caricature of Jia walking out of it, with a rainbow painted across.

"Too cliché?" she asked herself out loud. But drawing was the expression she knew.

She increased the volume of her already loud music. The playlist included more artists.

"Yes, Pa. I'll be ready at 6," she replied to his pending text. She had astonished Keshav and begun calling him Pa on his fiftieth birthday.

Jia's phone buzzed again. It was Sanya this time. She had met Sanya on a dating app and after a steady three years, Sanya had proposed. Jia could not say yes without confirming with Keshav.

"Have you told him yet?"

"*I'm gonna today* ..." Jia replied hastily.

Keshav reached the studio apartment she was living in after college had finished. Though it was a fully furnished flat, Jia had added touches of her eccentric self to the living room. She had covered the lights with colored paper, changing it every few days depending on her moods, and fairy lights twinkled across the room. She had a cactus she had named "Booh" after her old soft toy; she had two pictures placed on her TV cabinet – one with Smriti and one with Keshav.

He hadn't developed diabetes. In fact, he had lost some of his belly fat. And his smile was still a wonder.

"*Come down, I've reached,*" he texted as he reached her apartment.

Jia was dressed in a long white off-shoulder dress. Her curls kissed her slim shoulders. She wore minimal make-up.

She was fidgety. *God, help me.*

"You're nervous today, what happened?" Keshav smiled. His daughter was turning into a beautiful young lady. He had watched her go from a despairing teenager to a strong adult, managing her affairs beautifully.

"Let's reach the restaurant, we'll miss our reservation if we begin talking here," Jia replied.

As they walked into their favorite restaurant as regulars and ordered the usual with a nod to the attendant, Jia fetched out the caricature from her sling bag.

She was nervous. Though he was not her real father, he meant every bit the same to her. His heart was where her home lay, and with every passing day, she had been surer of it.

Her eyes were pinned on Keshav. He picked up the drawing. She was skipping beats, waiting for him to understand.

"But I don't understand, what are you trying to say?" Keshav said out aloud, bewildered. "Why are you walking out of a cupboard? And why is there a rainbow behind the cupboard?"

"OMG, you Gen X's …" Jia whispered, scared, hoping that he would accept her for the person she was. "Pa, I like a girl," she submitted.

"OH," Keshav replied, stunned with the information, not knowing what to say next.

"And she likes me back," Jia went on.

Keshav was silent for few minutes.

Please snap out of it quickly, she thought, squinting her eyes, shaking her knees under the table.

"Hmm. Ok. Is it serious now?" Keshav did not know how to have the talk. He had watched Jia grow up. He had thought about her having a boyfriend someday, or even being married, but having a girlfriend … the thought had not crossed his mind.

"Yes, if you're okay with it, I'm going to say yes to being engaged." Jia's look shifted from nervous to hope filled glitter.

He was blank. He let the information sink in. Jia had had a girlfriend for a while. He did not know about it. And then he was upset.

"You're getting engaged and now you're telling me there is someone? Am I not worthy of meeting ... uh ... her?" Keshav shook his head.

"Sanya, Pa. Her name is Sanya. I'm sorry, but how was I supposed to I break it to you that I'm gay? It was hard."

"You're gay?" Keshav asked, surprised, ignorant of the sexual spectrum. "Then aren't you supposed to like boys? Don't gays like boys?"

"Oh no. Leave that okay. We don't need to give you a lesson on this." Jia looked at her intelligent father. "If you are okay, would you like to have dinner with us during the weekend?" Jia asked.

Keshav paused for a moment. *It's a lot to take.*

"Hmm. Okay." Keshav left it at that.

After a long day at work and dealing with "coming out", which she wasn't sure Keshav understood perfectly, Jia was starving. She picked up her chopsticks and dug in like no one was watching.

"He's halfway there. Dinner on Saturday," Jia texted Sanya after dinner.

Keshav invited them for dinner, making sushi rolls which he had perfected by now, and ordered in the rest of the meal since making sushi took away all his time.

Keshav opened the door to see Sanya and Jia standing before him.

"Hi," Sanya greeted Keshav.

Keshav nodded in response.

Why isn't he smiling enough? Jia thought. She entered and pounced on the sofa.

Sanya sat along too. Keshav brought them the sushi rolls.

"I'm going to eat, you guys do the awkward chatting," Jia mumbled, picking up her chopsticks and diluting the wasabi in the soy.

"What do you do for a living?" he asked Sanya, skeptical and thinking what to ask a girl.

Are these the right questions for a girl? I was prepared for a boy! Keshav thought, irritably.

"I studied chartered accountancy in India, and now I am working here in Singapore, Sir."

"CA! You fell in love with someone who breathes and eats finance?" Keshav cried out.

Jia and Sanya looked at one another and laughed.

After chatting for an hour in a half-awkward, half-fun fashion, Keshav laughed too.

Thank you, God, thank you! Jia prayed.

The evening drew to a close, and he said goodbye to the two girls at the doorstep.

"Pa, will you get us married, then?" Jia asked with starry eyes, and Keshav's eyes were filled. He turned away, waving his hand. "Go away, now, you two."

***

In the following months, Keshav took Jia shopping for her bridal *lehenga*, booked the venue for dinner, and fixed caterers. He put his work on the backseat and planned Jia's wedding. They found a Hindu priest who would not mind performing ceremonies for a same-sex wedding. They arranged for him to fly down from the US.

A week before the wedding, Lata flew down to assist with the wedding preparations. She handed over Smriti's jewelry to Jia.

"You're old enough to take care of your belongings now," Lata said, placing the necklace on her bony neckline and a small *maang tikka* on her forehead.

Jia looked at herself in the mirror and then at Lata.

"Thank you, Lata Aunty, for everything." Jia hugged her and cried. Lata's eyes were wet too. "Smriti would be so proud of you."

In an intimate summer affair, with the *mandap* decorated with jasmine flowers, Jia was set to marry Sanya. Sanya had a small baraat ceremony with her many friends, parents, and relatives dancing in it. And Jia's few friends and Keshav's colleagues, and friends, waited to welcome the baraat. Mahesh had flown down with Yashna too.

"Smriti's daughter has landed right in front of you?" Mahesh asked Keshav. "You're getting Smriti's daughter married?"

"Yes Mahesh, exactly that," Keshav replied. "Hi Yashna, have you gotten accustomed to his jokes already?"

"I have, Keshav. Congratulations on the wedding," Yashna replied, grinning.

"I'm on the topic bro, don't divert. Smriti passed away, then Smriti's daughter ended up in Singapore to be mentored by you, and now you're getting her married!" Mahesh ventured.

"That's right. I've got to check on Jia, Mahesh. I hope you two enjoy the wedding," Keshav said.

Chung had flown in from Boston. She walked into the room where Jia was getting ready.

"Oiiii, Jia!" Chung looked at her. "You look so beautiful."

Jia looked at her with a slant head. "Chung, you've come!"

"Of course, I had to." Chung now had an American accent. "Listen, can I please flirt with Kav? He's right outside. I have a huge crush on him."

Jia grinned, "Go ahead. But hey, don't break my brother's heart."

Avantika was Jia's bridesmaid. She put the maang tikka on Jia's forehead. "Didi, we have to drape your *dupatta* now."

"Thanks, Avu." Jia nodded.

"Didi, can I take a selfie with you?" Avantika asked.

Jia nodded. The two of them pouted and posed.

"Sanya is ready for you, Jia," came Kaveer's voice from outside. "Her baraat is here."

Jia looked at the mirror and blushed.

Keshav walked into the room.

They looked at one another. Keshav blinked, and a tear rolled down his cheek.

"Are you ready?" Keshav asked.

Jia met his gaze. Keshav held her hand. "Your hands are cold … Are you feeling cold?"

Jia shook her head. He rubbed her hand between his palms.

"You know something… I had proposed to Smriti," Keshav told her.

"Wow, you had?"

"Yeah."

"She never got to be a bride …" Jia said, fiddling with her wedding ring. Her eyes welled up.

"No, no, Jia, don't cry …" Keshav said, lifting her face. "She'd be so proud of you."

If love were a venue, it was their hearts. If love was a scene, it was there, then, and them.

"Hey, her make-up will smudge!" Avantika yelled. "I was in the bathroom for two minutes and you've undone our hard work. Keshav Uncle, *chalo*, wait outside. And no more senti stuff!"

"By the way Pa, who proposes in two months? Both of you were the same!" Jia teased Keshav as Avantika pushed him outside the room.

Avantika draped Jia's dupatta over her head, pulling back her curls and tucking them in a puff.

She walked Jia outside and gave her hand to Keshav. He kissed Jia's forehead.

Jia held his warm hand and walked down to where Sanya was. The music played fainter than her heartbeat. She glanced at him, and then at Sanya.

As they took the *pheras*, sunlight entered her. All her screaming dungeons had healed.

In the reception that followed, Keshav took Jia in his arms for their first dance. He hugged her and swayed with the music.

"My pretty daughter," Keshav said, twirling her.

"I miss Mumma," Jia said, burying her face in his chest.

"Smriti told me that we will be together in another life. Jia, you are her other life. Our dear *Remembrance* lives on in you …"

ACKNOWLEDGEMENTS

Shiva, Guruji, Nanak: you hold me in unimaginable ways.

Kshitij, Harshinder, Suhani, Apurva, Nimrat, Paras, Pragya, Keeshwar, Vallabhi, Amisha, and Rashmeet masi, your honest feedbacks have uplifted the manuscript.

My parents and Awal, for your unconditional support; Veda, for her kisses. Nonah Khanna, for being my chosen family and my strength.

The Nu Voice Press team for bringing this work to culmination and Penguin Random House for taking it to the world.

AUTHOR'S BIO

❖

Kritika G Soin, a Chartered Accountant, transitioned from her corporate career to be an author, entrepreneur, and a start-up mentor. She has published two novels – *Mirror Soul* and *Vanilla Loves & Dusky Lives.* Her short story has been published in *Kitaab*, Singapore, a poem, in *Undiscovered Journal*, and a research article, in *Scientific God Journal*, USA. She was nominated for IFP's 2024 Mini-series Award, and nominated for TOI's Women's AutHer Award. She spoke at the Ananke Women Literature Festival 2024. She enjoys writing about romance, society, and spirituality. She has a garment enterprise by the name of KIYAH. In the capacity of an entrepreneur, she has judged pageants and been the official partner for Mrs. Rajasthan for four years. In the capacity of a mentor, she has counselled entrepreneurs at incubation centres for six years. She has also judged college events.